TWO THOUSAND GRUELING MILES

L. J. MARTIN

WOLFPACK
PUBLISHING
— EST 2013 —

*Dedicated to my sons, daughters' in law,
and grandchildren including those with 'step'
proceeding the title...love you one and all.*

TWO THOUSAND
GRUELING MILES

"You're a stinky toad," my little sister, Willy, yells at me. She's mad as I said she couldn't take the old rocking crib that once held me and my sisters and now is home to her rag dolls. I truly hope no one will have need of a crib in the months to come. The Oregon Trail is likely no place for a newborn, or for the Ma having to care for one.

"And you're a slimy tadpole," I reply, and she sticks her tongue out at me, which makes me laugh and her stomp away.

"What did you say to her?" my older sister, Edna Mae, yells from her perch stowing things in the wagon that's to be our home for some time.

"I told her she was pretty as a corn flower," I say, and laugh again.

"Horse feathers!" Edna Mae yells back, but goes back to her chore.

My Pa, Jedediah Tobias Zane, strides up from working on the wagon's front axle, which will receive the tongue, and says in that gravelly voice of his, "Here, Jake. Prove your worth." He hands me an adze and challenges me with a hand on my shoulder and those cold gray eyes appraising me.

I have hopes to grow another four inches in height to match his six feet, and weight to match his two hundred hard pounds. But even more than height and weight, I hope to acquire courage to match his. He's handing me tools for the job of work he's about to entrust me with.

"You'll be proud, Pa. May take me some days, but you'll be proud."

"It will be done in two days, son. Has to be. This is Thursday and we're leaving for Independence to train-up on Monday come sun-up."

"For sure, Pa?"

"Hell or high water, son. And don't tell your Ma I cursed."

"Yes, sir."

There is nothing in my life I want more than to make my father proud, and I will or my name is not Jacob Tobias Zane.

My fourteenth year, the first of last year—the fifth year we've been residents of St. Joseph, Missouri—and was one my Ma and Pa watched carefully. I turned fifteen in July and will turn sixteen while on the Oregon Trail.

During last year there wasn't a *St. Joseph Dispatch* or crossing journal written by a former traveler that both my parents didn't read cover-to-cover.

Pa says 1850 was a year of great consequence to our United States.

Texas surrendered its claim to New Mexico.

California was admitted as a state—Pa said only because it was proving to be laden with gold.

Congress was embroiled in fiery debates over slavery and states' rights. Much of what was published was read to us three children—not that Edna Mae or I considered ourselves children any longer—or handed to us with instructions to carefully read. In January of last year, 1850, Whig senator Henry Clay of Kentucky, introduced a so-called compromise and the year's events kept the local newspaper busy. But, even with the compromise, the argument over slavery continues. Ma said Congress is like a bunch of hogs fighting and slobbering over the trough.

And President Zach Taylor, the tough old general of the Mexican War who was quickly elected to head the country after Mexico surrendered, died after only a little more than a year in office. Taylor was a Virginia slave owner, which Pa said made the south happy, but Millard Fillmore, his vice president, who took over after Taylor's death, is a New Yorker. He is not a slave owner, and the south suddenly got real nervous.

The problem is our United States has acquired so much land from whipping the Mexicans we've almost doubled our size. The squabbling is over slave or free territory and the status of new states likely to be formed in all that new land.

Slave states are threatening to leave the Union if'n they don't get their way, and Pa says that could mean war—brother against brother is how he puts it.

And he wants his family to have nothing to do with it. None of it.

Pa says the North will never allow the South to leave the

Union—not only because of their opposition to slavery. Cotton is king in the South and southern states cotton is the second largest economic resource in the whole world. Without cotton, the USA will not be the envy of the world she's become. Pa says the North is a bunch of hypocrites, and the South is evil for owning human beings. He wants to get as far from Washington D.C. and the coming squabble as possible.

Ma says Pa really only wants to head west to grub in the mud for gold; Pa says it isn't mud on his hands that worries him but rather blood.

So, it's to be Oregon for the Zane family.

February, March, and the first half of April of this 1851, I've helped my Ma, Pa, and two sisters construct our transportation and gather and pack the dozens and dozens of items we've been advised we'll need for the coming adventure. Edna Mae, at seventeen, three years my senior, has spent her time sewing and mending—particularly sewing Mr. Goodyear's rubberized canvas sacks and sealing their seams with beeswax to waterproof them as much as possible for our dry goods. Willy—Wilhelmina—my younger sis, only twelve, has been assigned the duty of running errands for the rest of us and cooking our meals while Ma is busy administering and directing all of us. Pa accepts her direction, mostly, and only occasionally gets his hackles up and asserts himself as head of the family.

Ma is quietly seething about the coming trip as Pa, a saddle and harness maker by trade and a fair cobbler when called upon, has done well in St. Joe. Ma calls the adventure ahead "plunging into the maelstrom."

In addition to the plains wagon, we have one fine heavy cart, good for nearly a thousand pounds, which will be pulled by two mules. Mules will double as saddle animals on occasion when we're in camp. My saddle-maker father has built extra wide saddles for the mules' broad backs as they'll be ridden as well. Pa plans to hire a man to drive the cart. As he normally does, Pa traded harness he made for the mules. Some wagons I've seen pass have a small wagon pulled behind, called a pup, but Pa want's it separated, in case something happens to our larger plains wagon, and pulled by the mules as they're much faster than oxen—should speed become important at some time.

As well as gathering and packing, I'm helping Pa build, or I should say re-build, the heavy wagon that we'll call home in the coming months. Pa traded four saddles he'd built for a beat-up four-by-ten-foot grain wagon that has sound running gear and we've spent some weeks rebuilding it. It now has a new floor; thick three-foot high sideboards; a generous four-foot-wide-by three-foot-deep wagon box on the back; as well as narrow, one-by-one-foot, eight-foot-long boxes along nearly the full wagon length on the sides. All this has added weight, but light wagons, as reported by the journals we've read, have been known to blow over in the prairie winds.

Mr. Parker, the owner of the mercantile in town, owns a Peter Schuttler wagon, built in Chicago, and has allowed Pa to copy all those parts to improve our farm wagon. We've seen a few much larger Conestoga wagons pass, but Pa has read that the twenty-foot-long, unloaded, 3,500-pound wagons seldom make it far on the Oregon Trail. And those wagons require a minimum of six yokes of oxen. Our wagon will weigh only 1,200 pounds when empty and will be an easy load for three yokes at 3,000 pounds when loaded.

It's taken some time as we've caulked her and the cart, like boats, as we understand they may be used as such from time-to-time. We've also replaced all iron fittings with brass, where possible, as brass will not rust; and where not possible, we replaced what fittings we could with pegs. Still, our running gear is all bound with cast iron. Pa makes all the trees for his saddles and is a craftsman at pegging joints together. He even makes his own glue from hoof trimmings.

The plan is to pack oft-used items in a wagon box hanging off the back, line the interior with our dry goods and spares, then planks, then our bed clothes—flannel sheets, feather bed mattress, wool blankets—and other personal soft goods Edna Mae has packed in her sewn canvas sacks assigned to each with our name sewn on it. Tools and cooking implements will be hung outside, on the sides and bottoms of the wagon boxes. Those consist of a sheet-iron stove, a sixteen-inch Dutch oven, a long-handled twenty-inch cast iron frying pan, two light-weight tin pans, a flat twenty-four-inch square iron griddle, and implements.

Pa and I, who will hunt away from the train—it's reported trailside is hunted out—from time-to-time will carry small tin, cloth-covered, canteens for water. Hung forward on each side of the heavy wagon are twenty-gallon wooden kegs for water, and the cart carries another.

In addition to the brand-new Navy Colts we each have, we each also have a cap and ball rifle and shotgun. His, and one for a hired man we've yet to meet, are rifles of large .50

caliber; mine, a small .30 caliber. The three shotguns are 12 shot to the pound for Pa and the hired man; mine 20 to the pound for birds and small game. He's had me practice once a week, after Sunday service, for five months. I don't mind saying I'm nearly as good a shot as Pa is. Pa seldom misses anything with his rifle inside 100 paces, and at 200 will put it regularly inside a twenty-inch circle. If there is game, we won't go hungry for fresh meat. In case of emergency, both Ma and Edna Mae have become proficient with our firearms.

Chopping and shaping well cured hickory wood is not my favorite pastime, even with the praise of my father and my mother's promise of a cherry pie following the roasting of the chicken whose neck I wrung and rough-plucked just before Pa handed me the ax, adze, and plane.

The long, very strong log I'm working with ax and adze will be the wagon tongue, split on the end to fork the front axle, and will replace a smaller one that Pa found inferior. We've already replaced the axles with much heavier oak. A heavy chain will serve as primary trace and link the yokes of our oxen together beyond the first pair of wheel oxen.

Some wagons have as many as six yokes or twelve oxen. Pa has decided we need only three yokes. In addition to our six oxen we've been training for six months, we have three riding mules—two of which will pull the cart, two milk cows —Patches is the one freshened, Magda is one to be freshened on the trail—six beef steers, eight sheep, and a dozen chickens that will be carried in a two-foot-wide by six-foot-long by fifteen-inch-deep cage suspended beneath the wagon. As the cage is only six feet it leaves another two beyond each axle for belly bags, steer hides Pa has sewn with straps that, suspended beneath the wagon, will carry wood and buffalo chips we understand may be our only fire source for a good part of the trip. The chicken cage is a trick we learned from passing gypsies—ours will be occupied with White Pollock. The gypsies kept chickens of all colors so when they stole one as they passed a farm, the farmer couldn't pick his one from another. We'll enjoy their eggs until they stop laying, then their drumsticks and breasts.

The balance of the under-wagon space is my personal spot accommodating my sleeping hammock.

I have three feet of the twelve-foot tongue roughly shaped when my Pa slips up behind me while I'm wiping sweat from my eyes. As I'm concentrating so hard on the task, I don't hear him. I jump and almost drop my adze when he asks, "Jake, I'm off to town to buy the last of our goods." Then he laughs at me for jumping.

"You scared me, Pa."

"A man should be studying his work with his all. However, when we're on the plains, you'll need to be aware of all that goes on around you, as well as the task at hand. A rattlesnake might be in your path. An Indian in the bush. Your sheep or beef a'wanderin' off. Or God knows what. Now, would you like to ride in with me and help me load?"

"Yes, sir."

We've already sold the farm including most household goods, farm implements, our buckboard, the stock we're not taking, and Sunshine, our palomino mare—Pa says we've divested ourselves of hide, hair, bones and all. Ma says we've given away all they've worked for since being married.

2

As we'll need the buckboard wagon until we depart, its delivery to the buyer, Mr. Shaw, won't take place until just before we drive off toward Independence. There we're to meet up with Captain Cox and another two dozen families in the wagon train we've joined. Captain Cox, or so Pa has been convinced, is a wagon master who's made the Oregon trip twice before and knows every water hole and Indian hidey hole. Or so Pa has been told.

I may be a little more skeptical than Pa, as Ma and I wonder how a man could even begin to remember all for 2,000 miles of deserts, plains, and mountains. I guess we'll see.

Town, and Parker's Mercantile, is only a mile or so and we often go by foot, but it's two hundred pounds or so of goods we're to buy to add to the more than two thousand pounds we've packed, or soon will.

The large wagon is already eighteen inches deep in goods and only awaits a few more things. The wagon boxes are packed with tools and goods we'll use on a daily basis and emergencies, and the cart, with its four-by-six-foot, two-foot-deep bed is lined on the bottom with plowshares and tools, including Pa's draw-down table, a saddle maker's necessity. The chairs and Ma's spinning wheel are hung on the outside of the wagon, along with ax, adze, pots, and pans.

Shep, our herd dog and my best friend, is allowed to run along beside us until he tires and with an easy leap, clears the foot-high sideboards of the buckboard and shoves his head between us.

As we plod along, Pa hands me the list that he's been checking things off of for many months. By far, the majority of reminders have a line drawn through. One hundred fifty pounds of flour for each of us six—family and hired man. Half a bushel each of dry beans, peas, apples, peaches, and ten pounds of cornmeal. Ten pounds of salt, five pounds of coffee, two of tea, and condiments including a small keg of vinegar. Two pounds of saleratus to help our bread rise. Four months ago, we butchered eight of our hogs we didn't sell on the hoof and have packed four large hams, seventy-five pounds of bacon and fifty pounds of sausage that has been curing in our smokehouse since. And tools—hand saw, hammer, crosscut saw, small anvil, small leather bellows, and auger. Of course, we have spare horseshoes and nails for the mules.

And books. Ma insisted we take a dozen books so our studies can continue en route—Smith's First Book in Geography, First-Year Latin, Progressive First Reader, three volumes of McGuffey's Readers, a dictionary—Ma says we're to learn a new word every day—the Bible, and more. The dictionary is a big fat thing...an *American Dictionary of the English Language Exhibiting the Origin, Orthography, Pronunciation, and Definitions of Words* by Noah Webster. Maybe I'll learn what orthography means? Those and her spinning wheel, she said, would go or she wouldn't. Pa is taking his draw-down table, used in his saddle making, and a set of punches. They argued long and hard, each against the other taking those large items and finally agreed both would go. Ma wanted to take an oak table passed down to her from her mother, but Pa put his foot down. He did agree to take four spindle-back chairs—of the eight that matched the table. That all was a negotiation that went on for more than a week.

MacLean Parker, proprietor of the mercantile, is a friend of Pa's and along with Pa, they are deacons in our church. Mr. Parker's a bear of a man who I've seen carry a fifty-pound keg of nails under each arm and run up and down his plank stairs to load a wagon for a customer. He would not have to do so today as we're getting hardtack, hemp rope, gingham cloth, two gross of needles, tools to shear the sheep for raw wool that will occupy Ma and her spinning wheel. Wool doesn't weigh much. Pa has read the savages will value needles with large eyes as trade goods. We also load twenty pounds of dried, salted cod up from New Orleans, and a two-gallon keg of molasses.

The heaviest new items we are to load are two dozen ax heads, them also for trade goods, which, without handles, don't take up much room.

And hopefully a crock of hard candy Pa said he'd buy for us young'uns and to trade to the savages.

As we return home—me smiling as the crock of hard candy rides in the rear—Pa gets a little sentimental. "I truly hate to leave the farm, but I believe I'm doing the right thing for all of us."

"I know you're worried about Ma, but she'll come to your way of thinking. Edna Mae and Willy hate to leave their friends, but I'm the envy of mine, going to see the elephant and all."

Pa laughs. "You know that's merely a saying and there are no elephants, other than in some shows or zoos, in North America."

"I know, Pa. I graduated the eighth grade."

"And I'm proud of you for it and for the work you've done hence."

I give him a shy smile. "Proud enough to spare a piece of that hard candy you bought?"

He laughs again. "Ma made a pie and it won't keep till we get half way to Oregon. Hard candy will."

Reaching over, he messes my hair, a habit of his I dislike, but we both laugh.

When we rein up at our barn, he instructs me to unhitch, water and grain the mare Sunshine while he loads the wagon. Then we're to finish and set the tongue. I'd like to finish it myself, but Pa says he's eager to try the new harness out. Then we'll hook up our oxen, all three yokes, for the first time for a trail run.

But by the time we have the tongue shaped, it's supper time and Ma is calling us in.

I've noticed that as Pa says grace, it's getting longer and longer. There seem to be more worries he wants the Lord to keep from our path, from weather to Indians to lack of water and graze, to our good health. Finally, we eat.

And as I wonder about how good the meals will be on the trail, I can't help but stuff in fried chicken, mashed potatoes and gravy, green beans, fresh bread and applesauce and two full mugs of buttermilk.

Not to speak of a generous slice of Ma's pie.

As we eat quietly, I think on our oxen. Oxen are nothing more than cattle—bulls, that have been castrated at an early age and trained until four years of age to work in a yoke beside another bull and, along with other pairs, or yokes, to pull a wagon. Pa purchased and traded for ours and we've had them nearly a year. I've seen as many as nine yokes, or eighteen oxen pulling a pair of huge wagons and trailing a pup cart. Pa says three yokes will do for our large wagon.

Our mules are large and well trained. We've had two draft horses for as long as I remember, and Pa—long before we moved from Virginia to Missouri—bred them to a stallion said to be a Morgan and, then in turn, bred two half-draft half-Morgan mares to a neighbor's big jackass. A jack the neighbor, Hector Snodgrass, claims is a direct descendent of the mammoth jack imported to the country by no less than George Washington.

President Washington is said to be the father of America's mule industry. Pa doubts that ours is a direct descendent, but I spent some time in the St. Joseph library and learned our first president bred thousands of mules from a mammoth jack said to be from Andalusia and given him by Marquis de Lafayette, who fought with him during the revolution.

Anyway, we ended up with two matching sixteen-hand

mules bred and trained on our own places, and one fourteen-hand mule Pa purchased. The smaller animal is sort of mine, as I've ridden him since I was large enough to stand on a box and get a foot in the stirrup.

Pa named the mules Mark, as Marquis was too big a mouthful, and George.

My little fella we call Stubby.

I sleep well, considering I spent half the night dreaming of being chased by Indians and scalped.

As we finish a breakfast of flapjacks, honey, sidepork and fried eggs, someone knocks on our door hard enough that it rattles the table setting.

"That would be Sampson," Pa says, and hurries to the door.

Shep, who's at my feet as usual, growls low.

One of the biggest black men I've ever seen fills the doorway, hat in hand.

"Have you taken your meal?" Pa asks, and the man shakes his head.

I look back over my shoulder where Ma is clearing the table and am a little surprised to see her staring with mouth agape. I guess she hasn't met the man Pa hired to accompany us.

"Margaret, this is Sampson," Pa introduces them, then as an afterthought, "And our son Jake, and daughters Edna Mae and Wilhelmina—most call her Willy."

The huge man fills the doorway, hat in hand, until Ma shuts her mouth and hurries forward and grabs him by the upper arm—a bicep as big as my waist—and pulls him inside.

To my surprise, Shep stops growling and is wagging his

tail. He trots over and waits for Sampson to give his ears a scratch, and he does. Satisfied, Shep returns to my feet.

"Give Mr. Sampson your seat, Jake," Ma says, and I do. Sampson gives us each a nod and takes a chair. He takes up twice the table space I did. Both of my sisters are staring at the big man with the same surprise they might have had a full grown oak tree uprooted itself and shoved into our kitchen, seated itself, and rested huge limbs on the table.

Sampson is glancing around, seeming to be surprised that he's at the family table. I'm wondering if it's the first time he's ever been at a white folks table? My Ma and Pa have proven to be blind to folks of color, so I'm not surprised, but Sampson sure seems to be.

Ma has recovered her composure. "Girls, clear the table while I cook Mr. Sampson some vittles."

The big man still has not said a word, then Pa explains to all of us. "Sampson lost his tongue so he doesn't speak. He hears real good and we'll have to learn some of his sign language and ... and the meaning of the sort of grunts he does ... but he's a fine worker and a pious man, and we'll get on fine."

Ma quickly mixes up more batter and soon has a half dozen flapjacks almost round as the plate in front of the big man. He gives Ma a toothy grin as she sets molasses, peach jam, and a bowl of fresh-churned butter near. Then pours him a mug of buttermilk. Pa is pulling on his boots to return to the wagon tongue, when Ma finishes serving and turns to him. "Mr. Zane, I'd like to speak to you a moment," and heads for their bedroom without awaiting a reply.

Looking a bit apprehensive, Pa finishes lacing and tying his boots, then follows.

Mr. Sampson keeps his head down, concentrating on his flapjacks as the voices beyond the door rise in volume.

Until the last words I hear before Pa stomps out are, "... he's a freeman by his word, working for transportation and found, and needs to get the hell out of Missouri. He does the work of two men and that's the end of it."

As Pa comes through the bedroom door, Ma asks in a stern tone, "Of course, you've seen his manumission papers? And how does a mute man give his word?" I know a slave is freed by what's called manumission.

Pa turns back. "I take his word. And he gives it with a nod of his head, in answer to my inquiry." Then he slams the door behind and heads outside.

I've seldom heard voices raised between my parents but know things have been a bit stressful as of late.

Sampson is assigned a place to sleep in the barn, after he and Pa have finished the tongue and laid out the yokes, traces and chain.

Tomorrow, after our last visit to a St. Joseph church, we'll finish packing wagon and cart, test the rigging, then, on Monday morning, as Pa says, "God willing and the creek don't rise," we are off to see the elephant.

3

I'M LOOKING FORWARD TO SEEING SO MUCH I'VE READ ABOUT: lots of buffalo, antelope, elk and deer, if the journals I've read are true. And with luck, maybe a mountain lion and grizzly bear.

My Ma has not been in favor of this move, saying we are diving into the maelstrom. My older sis, Edna Mae, at seventeen years old has been stomping around angry when not stitching and sewing and readying. She's mad about having to leave her friends, and particularly one who she admitted to me she'd had eyes for, Johnny Peabody. And mad about selling our palomino which she considered hers, even if not. And my little sis, Willy—actually, Wilhelmina—is angry with me as well as I said she couldn't take the rocking crib that held the three of us at one time or another and now only has been crib for her half dozen rag dolls. The dolls, however, have found a place in the wagon.

Ma has Pa's Webster's and informs us that today's word is one she's used, maelstrom, and we have to each repeat its meaning, 'a large whirlpool in a body of water'. I asked her what that has to do with us falling into one on the prairie and she frowns and explains that sometimes words are used figuratively and metaphorically, not literally. So, I have to ask what metaphorically means and she walks away, saying, "tomorrow," over her shoulder.

Ma says as we're to learn a new word each day that when we arrive we'll be as smart as Ben Franklin or Thomas Jefferson. I happen to know Jefferson knew Greek and Latin, so I'd guess that's some exaggeration.

Only this morning did we set out with the wagon we've rebuilt and three yokes of oxen we've trained, being driven by Pa and, so far, preforming well.

Our new hired man, Sampson, is driving our cart, pulled by two sixteen-hand mules bred and trained by Pa. Sampson is mute due to the loss of his tongue—how, I haven't discovered as of yet, but hope to when I get his trust. He's hard to communicate with but smiles and laughs a lot, knows what needs doing and does the work of two. I think we'll be fine friends. Pa says Sampson has received his manumission and is a free man, but I think Ma doubts that as he has no papers. She thinks he's an escaped slave—he has scars on his wrists and ankles as if he's worn shackles at some time—and it concerns her that slave hunters from as far away as Mississippi may be on his trail. Even if so, I hope he stays with us and we help him fight shy of trouble.

Stubby, a little fourteen-hand mule, is mine to ride and, with Shep's help, to herd the six steers, two milk cows, and half dozen sheep accompanying us. Them, and the dozen chickens suspended in a cage under the main wagon—and hunting—should keep us in fresh meat the whole five months we expect to spend on the Oregon Trail.

With both my sisters afoot with walking sticks doubling as pokes to move the stock along, and me riding Stubby with a six-foot whip Pa wove for me, we're able to keep the stock moving. As we've only been on the road for half a day and about to stop for lunch, the stock has yet to get into the rut of moving along together. Driving steers, cows, and sheep, we're discovering, is a little like trying to herd cats. I'm sure it will get better. At least I hope it will. Thank the Lord, Pa has allowed me to bring my pup, Shep, along. I convinced Pa about Shep as it seems he can sniff out a rattlesnake at twenty paces. Him smelling them out is way better than one of us stepping on one. As long as he doesn't get nose bit. But I think he's too smart for that.

So far, each time the stock see or smell a spring-green plush meadow, they want to wander that way.

It's a little frustrating to set out on a long, long journey, and begin by going the wrong direction. We should be heading west, but rather are going south to meet up with the Horatio Cox Oregon-or-Bust wagon train. Pa has been corresponding with Captain Cox and sent a bank draft of one hundred dollars as application fee. We're to join the train in Independence, sixty-five miles south of our farm near St. Joseph, and only then turn west.

Although Independence is east of the Missouri River, Pa elected to ferry across and go south on the west side of the river—he's a friend of the St. Joe ferry master and gets a cheap rate—then ride a mule or take the cart over to the site picked for forming up the wagon train near the town of Independence. He's been told there are two dozen families or more who'll move together, work together for the over two thousand miles of trail we'll face.

As the stock are finally moving together, seeming to begin to get the idea, I offer to walk and let Edna Mae ride. Pa has made a beautiful sidesaddle so the ladies can ride as a woman is expected to, but it's packed in the cart.

"I'll walk if you want to try and sit without your saddle," I offer, and she nods.

I help my older sis into perching with both legs on the left, or mounting side, of Stubby, with only one foot in a stirrup.

"When do I ride?" Willy runs up to us and asks.

"Climb up beside Sampson. He'll let you ride along."

"I want to ride Stubby."

I laugh. "You afraid of Sampson?"

Sampson has overheard me and looks over and grunts, which is about all he can do. He pouts a big bottom lip out as if his feelings are hurt, and that gains a laugh from Edna Mae and me.

"I ain't afraid of nothin'," Willy says, and crosses her arms adamantly.

"I'm not afraid of anything," Edna Mae corrects.

"Me neither," Willy says, and Edna Mae and I both guffaw, knowing she didn't understand she was being corrected.

"Willy," I say with a smile, "you stomp along with your arms crossed and you'll trip and break that pointy beak of your'n."

"An' you're still a toad," she snaps, and stomps on ahead

until she's even with the big wagon where Ma is perched high beside Pa, who works the reins.

"You should know, tadpole," I call after her.

We are three days—beginning to get into the necessity of things—on the road south and it seems Ma and Pa are not getting on well. I'm thinking it's because Ma didn't want to go on this trip at all. But then I can't help but overhear their conversation when I draw up close behind, easily walking faster than the oxen, while Willy is riding Stubby and Edna Mae is poking the stock along.

"How can you be so sure?" I hear Pa ask.

"Doesn't matter, Jed. She spent near the whole night out and there's nothing we can do about it now."

"She denies ... denies letting him have his way with her?"

"Over and over. Said they just spent the night talking because she was leaving for Oregon. She said she hoped he'd ask her to marry and she could stay in Missouri, but he didn't."

"As God is my witness," Pa says, and his tone is harsh, "I should put her over my knee and pound her backside for a week."

"Who the devil is this black heart who'd defy our trust?"

"Jed, it's your own daughter. Johnathan Peabody is the boy. And he's a nice enough lad from a nice family."

"Nonetheless, I should beat him silly."

"If you'll recall, sir, I climbed out a window to be with you more than one time. Just pray she's telling the truth."

"Like you say, nothing we can do now, nothing but beseech the good Lord."

I drop back, not wanting them to know I overheard.

It seems my older sister, Edna Mae, is the subject of the conversation, and likely the cause of what I thought was a different reason for the sparks flying between my folks for the last three days. I had no idea she'd spent a night away from home, but as she had her own room and window, sneaking out was easily done. Seems Ma found her out, and I'm surprised Ma dressing her down wasn't heard all over the farm.

It is late the third night when we reach the ferry on the west side of the Missouri, across from Independence, and I walk with Pa from our campsite to talk with the ferryman. He negotiates the cart and all she'll carry crossing for only a half dollar, the same price as for man and horse, so long as he's ready to cross at sun-up. I see there are two competing ferries, so Pa mentioned to the ferryman he could try the competition. They shake and we return to camp. Pa and Sampson hobble the mules and stake out Hercules, our lead ox, while I haul water from the river two buckets at a time. The ladies busy themselves fixing us stew and biscuits. My last chore is milking the freshened cow, and a quart and a half goes into the fresh churn—we have a small churn for fresh and one for sour milk.

We've made almost twenty-three miles this day walking, poking the stock along, and riding some. So, after filling my stomach with stew, sourdough biscuits—Ma is very good with the everlasting dough—and my spoonful of honey for the day, I sleep dry and warm in my hammock rolled in a canvas under our big plains wagon. Ma, Pa, and the girls are comfy inside. Sampson snores away in the cart, under its canvas cover with his tree-trunk-size calves hanging over the back.

Tomorrow we meet our wagon master, Captain Horatio Cox, and the rest of the families on the train. I truly hope there's some young folks my age.

And that all of us get along as it'll be an extra-long trip if not.

4

SINCE HE COULD TAKE THE CART FOR THE SAME PRICE AS going alone, Pa invited me to ride along. I was, I admit, second choice as he asked Sampson first, and Sampson adamantly shook his head. Him not wanting to go into town seemed to make Ma worry even more that Sampson had something to hide.

It took us two hours to locate our party a couple of miles south of Independence where they were gathered, wagons in a circle.

I could hear a gruff voice yelling as we circled several oxen grazing the pasture grass outside the circle of covered wagons. Pa tipped his hat at a pair of mounted men guarding the herd, but I could see he was playing close attention to what was going on ahead. Pa ground-tied the mules outside the circle of wagons and I followed him as he jumped a tongue and moved through some ladies and kids—all facing the ruckus—and headed to a group of men near a campfire. Beyond them as many or more mules and oxen as outside, and a few horses, were gathered inside the circle of wagons around piles of mowed meadow grass.

"By God you'll dump half that pile of trash or you won't be in this party," the same gruff voice I'd heard before, I see now is attached to a man nearly as big as Sampson but with a six-inch bushy black beard and a head of hair equally black, bushy, and long.

He has a stubby finger in the chest of a man equally tall but broomstick thin.

"What'll it be?" he asks the man.

"It'll be my hundred dollars back, that's what."

"I reserved your spot in the train with that hundred, pilgrim. They ain't gonna be no refunds."

I see the skinny man's face redden and he looks as if he's a steam engine about to blow.

The skinny man wears a revolver, as does bushy, and has a hand resting on the butt. He takes a step back, out of the big man's reach, before he spits his words. "By God, I'll have my money back or you'll wet this ground with your blood."

He has the revolver lifted only an inch when an equally tall man, weight somewhere between the skinny and the bushy man, steps out of the crowd behind and smashes the skinny man upside the head with his heavy revolver.

The skinny man folds like a pair of long johns that had been blown off Ma's clothesline. Blood spurts from the side of his head.

Shep, who's been quiet at my side, growls and barks, and backs away but stays between the fallen man and the one who hit him, and me.

The fellow who'd felled the skinny fella is a brindle-topped man with a face rusted with freckles. His teeth are as black as the bushy man's beard and one of his eyes light blue as river ice—the other white and bumpy as curdled cow's milk with a reddened scar across it. I can't help but notice how filthy his knotted hands are, and his shirt and trousers are little cleaner, if any.

Just looking at him makes my back shiver and my stomach go sour, and what he did makes my mouth go dry.

"You might'a kilt him, Duffy," bushy says, "... not sure that was called for." He's looking dubious with a cock of his head and a frown and furrowed brow.

"Him or you, Cox, he was reaching and everyone knows it was self-defense," the redhead says, then turns to the other men in the group. "Somebody fetch his woman and some of you carry this pile of crap to his wagon."

Four men step out of the crowd, hoist the skinny man and move off.

Pa rests a hand on my shoulder. "Go back to the cart and wait for me."

"Yes, sir," I say, but I only take two steps back.

Pa strides over to the bushy man, who I now presume is our wagon master, Mr. Cox, and steps up near the two of them but carefully not turning his back on the redhead.

"I'm Zane. I presume you're Wagon Master Cox."

"I am," the big man says, and sticks a thick paw out to shake.

They do, then Cox motions to the redhead with a nod. "This here is Red McDuff. Duffy is number two in command. Where's your wagon? I've inspected the others and you're the only one left."

"Other side of the Missouri. Ferryman wanted three dollars to bring it, my cart, and my critters over. Then it would have been three back the other way. I figured you could inspect when the train gets across."

The big man furrows his brows and glares at Pa.

"Look, pilgrim, we was to meet here and not begin until I'd approved all the wagons and stock. You ain't getting off to much of a good start."

"But if you approve my rig, on the other side of the river, I'll be six dollars ahead and if I'm to pay you the other two hundred I owe, it would likely be good I had the coin to do so."

"Don't tell me all you got is the rest of the fee? You'll need …"

"Mr. Cox," Pa interrupts. "I don't guess you need to know how much I might have. Truth be known, I have enough to get to Oregon then some."

"Zane, you said. Well, Mr. Zane, you're a sassy sort and I don't know that we'll get on …"

Again, Pa interrupts him. "Don't much matter we get along, Mr. Cox. What matters is you do what you say and promised, and so do I. And I always do exactly what I say I'll do as faithful as the sun rising in the east."

Cox stares at my Pa for a moment, then asks, "Seems you're a saddle and harness man, if'n I remember."

"I am—and a cobbler of some skill."

"Then I'll not throw you out like I would a busted axle. I'll take a look at your rig on the far side of the river. You be ready to pay up in gold coin if'n I approve."

"See you across the river," Pa says, and spins on his heel

and starts back, giving me a hard, disapproving look as he comes.

"Zane!" The redheaded man, Duffy, calls out to Pa who stops and turns.

"That's the last time you'll sass Mr. Cox, or you'll answer to me."

Shep begins to growl and I'm pretty sure he doesn't think much of Duffy.

I can see Pa's hands at his sides go to fists. "Mr. Duffy, or McDuff, or whatever your name might be, you should know that I answer to God and my wife, in that order. Should you, Mr. Cox, and I disagree on something to do with the trip, then all you'll get is a nod from me and mine. If it's something other than what you're paid to be expert in, then we'll find a way to settle our differences."

"Humph," Duffy says, but makes no move forward.

Pa gives them both a nod. "Gentlemen," he says, and spins on his heel and pushes me ahead.

"Mr. Cox don't seem to be much of a gentleman," I say.

Shep, as I've noticed him do when trouble raises its ugly head, stays between us and it.

"He doesn't have to be, 'cept around your Ma," Pa says and ruffles my hair, which is not my favorite thing. The he adds, "All Captain Cox has to do is get us to Oregon safe and in one piece."

"That all?" I say, and that makes Pa chuckle sardonically.

IT's midmorning when the train begins to arrive on our side

of the river, two wagons and miscellaneous stock on each flat boat for the crossing.

Mr. Cox is first off the ferry, riding a tall, steel gray, hammer-headed sixteen-hand horse that prances as if he's in a Fourth of July parade.

Cox moves quickly covering the two hundred yards to our camp at a lope. We have both wagon and cart fully harnessed and ready—Ma perched on the wagon with reins in hand. Sampson sits on the cart, his head hanging and his big-brimmed floppy hat pulled low over his eyes.

As soon as Mr. Cox's feet hit the ground, Pa is next to him, smiling, hand extended. It is plain to me that Pa wants this journey started on a good footing with Mr. Cox. Cox isn't smiling, but he is cordial with his handshake. Then he walks directly to the plains wagon, bends and looks carefully at the running gear, then stands, frowning.

"This ain't no wagon I know anything about and though it looks like a Schuttler, it ain't. You build this yourself?"

"I did and it's more stout than a Chicago Schuttler. I had one to copy, and did, except you'll note there're some brass fittings that won't rust, and where Schuttler is bolted with iron, which will rust. I've hardwood pegged and glued ...."

"Pegs'll loosen and she'll fall apart," Cox interrupted.

"Not my pegs. I've been making saddletrees and repairing buckboards and wagons for many years and never had a complaint yet nor a failure."

"And you've never ridden or driven one two thousand miles, eighteen hundred miles of which don't know a road from a road apple."

"Both my wagon and cart are sound as any wagon built, and as any boat as they're caulked to float."

"Humph," Cox says. "I guess it's your hide and that of your'n should she fall apart. Don't expect me to risk the train should you have to lay out to rebuild for more than a day and not that if more than once. Understand?"

"You want the rest of your money?"

"I do."

"How's that thin fellow that Mr. McDuff beat down?"

"Died in the night."

"A pity." Pa's tone lowers an octave and I must listen closely to hear. "Mr. Cox, that was none of my business, but it doesn't set well with me."

"Mr. Zane, I'm the wagon master and judge, jury, and executioner on this journey. How does that set with you?"

"Doesn't matter to me who judges, Mr. Cox. As long as it's fair and square."

"Then fetch up the rest of my money and get ready to fall in line. You're last to be inspected, so you'll fall in at the rear."

Mr. Cox has totally ignored Ma and the girls, and Sampson and me, until he is ready to mount up. Then, after pocketing his money, he turns back to Pa.

"I'm not fond of Nigras on my trains. You tell your man ...."

"He's his own man," Pa snaps.

"You tell your man to mind his manners. I see him look crossways at one of the ladies and I'll hang him from the first stout oak we find."

"He's a gentleman; and he's his own man."

"Humph," Cox groans, and mounts, kicking rocks up behind as he gallops away.

Ma leans out from the wagon seat. "Mr. Zane, it's a fine fella you picked to travel with."

"So long as he knows what he's doing and gets us safely through the wilderness, he's fine enough for my taste."

"I guess a wager would be out of the question," Ma says, but doesn't wait for an answer and disappears back into the wagon.

This just might be even a longer trip than we thought.

5

SOME HILLS, BUT NOT MANY. SOME TREES, IF YOU LOOK HARD and shade your eyes. Except in the cuts where there's a stream bed.

Kansas, that's what many are calling this part of the undeveloped area—Pa calls it Indian territory—and we're headed northwest across the northeast corner of the area that's said has been laid out to be that state. If it passes Congress. In a day or two we'll be in the part of the undeveloped area some are calling Nebraska. All of it, and lots more west of the Missouri, became U.S. territory when we whipped the Mexicans. Most of this huge belly of the country is so-called 'unorganized' territory, stretching from our home state of Missouri across the plains and deserts to where it touches New Mexico territory, Utah territory, and Oregon territory on the west—where we're headed—with Canada on the North and Texas on the south. Beyond Utah and New Mexico territories lays the brand new state of California. Pa said California was quickly approved as it's said to be laden with gold. It's said Congress also hurried California's approval so the U.S.A. would be from ocean to ocean across the continent, which would discourage the English who have designs on the west coast.

I can see a long way in this flat un-treed country. Other than waving prairie grass, what I see most, that's moving, is wagons—a line of covered wagons as far as I can see, like white dung beetles creeping across the green prairie, but I hope we're hunting something better than a pile of scat.

Our family group, one of two dozen in our train, is a covered wagon and cart. Ma, Pa, older sis Edna Mae, younger sis Willy, me in the middle, and hired man Sampson plus fourteen head of steers, milk cows, and sheep. Many wagons have as many or more of each.

Pa is surprised to discover that Sampson, our new hired man, is as good with the oxen as Pa is himself. The days are long when doing the same job for hours, so Pa has traded off. At the beginning of each day, Pa drives the big wagon, our four-by-ten-foot rebuilt farm wagon now covered with canvas over arched hickory. Then he trades and drives our four-by-seven-foot mule-pulled cart and Sampson takes over the plains wagon and three yokes of oxen. Sometimes I'm allowed to drive the cart and two mules, but mostly I ride Stubby, our short fourteen-hand mule. Mounted on Stubby, I shepherd our two milk cows, six steers, and six sheep that will be our meat supply if absolutely necessary and, if not, the beginning of new herds on our land claim in Oregon. Pa hopes we'll get to Oregon with at least one cow to breed and one steer we can trade for a bull to begin a new herd, as well as a ewe and ram.

Pa is six feet tall and two hundred or more pounds, the last time he weighed on the grain scale at the feed store in St. Joseph, our kicking-off place and home for more'n five years. Sampson is a massive Nigra man, taller that Pa by an inch or two, and closer to three hundred pounds than two. He's half a head taller and twice the weight of the average man. Sampson, a mute, is missing a good part of his tongue. Pa thinks Sampson was a slave and some heathen plantation owner likely cut Sampson's tongue out for back-talking him. When I'm a better friend of Sampson's, I'll broach the subject with him. I caught him reading, which is somewhat a surprise as most of the slaves, at least in the slave state of Missouri, can't read or write as it's illegal to teach one to do so. If Sampson can read, most likely he can write, and we'll communicate much easier.

Ma has still not warmed up to the huge man and when Pa calls him forward to trade drivers Ma either walks or rides the cart with Pa. The constant rocking of the wagon and cart on the rutted trail makes some doze and some downright seasick, and walking is a welcome diversion.

It's still spring, so we've had the occasional rain. Consequently, the dust is hardly noticeable yet, even though we're at the rear of our train of now twenty-six wagons. The train ahead of us seems to be at least fifty wagons—if it's all one group—and the one behind nearly that. They've stayed back a mile or so, and we've stayed a half mile behind the train in front. It seems two wagons have already dropped out—or been thrown out—of other trains and joined with us. We started out with only two dozen.

With the other groups ahead and behind seeming to be at

least twice our size, it makes me wonder about the organizer of our group. Maybe there's a reason folks didn't want to train up with him?

Captain Horatio Cox, our wagon master, and my Pa got off to a rough start as Cox and his number two, McDuff, a rawboned redhead with a rusty complexion, beat that man to death where we trained up. They called it self-defense. Pa seems doubtful. At least I think McDuff is freckled, but it may be dirt as he's a filthy man. I've thought on this a lot—wandering along gives one lots of thinking time—and I think it an evil thing they did. The more I think on it, the more it seems a murder. And Mr. Cox and filthy Duffy worry me considerable.

We've only had a few nights on the trail as a train, starting early and camping late, so we haven't mingled much. It seems to me Cox and his man, McDuff, who goes by Duffy, don't encourage the families to mingle. Since we're yet to be in serious Indian country, we have yet to circle up and just camped hodgepodge along the trail when it got dark. When we do circle up, head-to-tail with others, we should get to know them all.

Our third day and Pa is pleased with the way both wagon and cart are performing.

It's only a little after four when Red McDuff gallops along the train and informs us we're to circle up near a little stream only a mile or so ahead and that there will be a gathering, a train meeting, at 7:00 p.m. after we've supped and taken care of our stock. As we approach, I see two other trains are already circled nearby with smoke from a large bonfire snaking up; and the train behind is coming on. Looks as if we'll have a regular city of wagons.

We're four hundred yards south of the main crossing and I'm a little surprised to find the ground grazed off. I drive our stock a mile farther south, with Sampson's fine company. He's saddled George, one of our big mules, and joined me. He teaches me a game while we relax and watch the oxen, mules, six steers, two cows, and six sheep graze. Paper, rock, and scissors is a simple game, but we get lots of laughs as my paper covers his rock or his scissors cut my paper. You get to whack the other guy's wrist with two fingers when you win. I can't hit the big man hard enough to make him wince and, thank goodness, he doesn't more than sting me a little.

A little farther down the creek we find a couple of small trees that have fallen, floated, and been left high and dry by receding water. Both of us carry thirty feet of line tied to saddles, so we kick the smaller limbs away from the trunks and rope and drag them back for firewood—already getting to be a rare commodity on the trip. Next time we tote ax and adze along.

When we return, I just have time before supper to milk our one freshened cow and add the quart and a half to Ma's fresh churn.

As I'm pouring milk into the fresh churn, I advise Edna Mae that unless she wants to drive the stock to graze and fetch wood, the milking is her chore from now on and before she can complain, Ma agrees. Edna Mae bites her tongue, then sticks it out at me when Ma turns away.

The creek sort of runs north and south, snaking around, and we're the most southerly of the camps. Ma has had the foresight to be soaking beans to soften since morning and cooks them up with a fat chunk off one of the hams, biscuits done in the Dutch oven, and good water from the creek that still runs pretty high—but not so high we have any worries about crossing.

Eating quickly, I ask to be excused and wander over to where folks are gathering for the meeting. One old white-haired gentleman is bowing a fiddle, and it's a gay sound that makes me smile. He's soon joined by a man with a mouth harp. We're all tapping our toes when Captain Cox gives a shout and we quiet down.

I count the folks we're travelling with when we're all on our butts in the grass in the center of the wagons. There are one hundred thirty of us, including Captain Cox and McDuff. One family has eight folks, including grandma and five youngsters. Then I realize another five young men have been assigned to guard the stock that are gathered south of the circle, but not as far south as I've taken ours to graze. Two of the wagons are made up of only two folks, a pair of brothers on one and a pair of newlyweds not much older than Edna Mae's seventeen on the other. My new count of folks in the company is one hundred thirty-five. And, by the looks of a three of the ladies, we'll add at least three more on the journey. That'll make a hundred and thirty-eight, presuming we don't lose anyone before we add.

I'm not feared of much, but sickness seems a thing you can't fight and cholera has run rampant through some of the trains, or so rumor has said.

A few folks are still chattering, most having only just met. We're all racked to dead silence when Captain Cox draws and fires his revolver in the air. But we're also suddenly attentive.

"By God," he growls, "when I say seven I mean seven and you'll all stop your palaverin' and pay attention when that minute hand, should you have watches or clocks, hits the high point. Do you understand?"

No one objects, in fact most nod.

"Now," he commands, "not a squeak unless I call on you."

Pa and the rest of our family, other than Sampson, have walked up beside me. I'm not surprised with Pa standing adamantly. He doesn't nod or reply but has never taken to being talked down to. He folds his arms and furrows his brow at Cox and McDuff. But he says nothing sharp to either of the train bosses, and, to be truthful, I'm glad he doesn't.

My father wouldn't like me repeating it, but as I stand next to him in the growing darkness, with the campfire making Captain Cox's face flash like he is Satan himself, Pa whispers "you sonofabitch." Then he clamps his jaw.

Shep gives him a growl, then stays between him and us as we walk away.

6

Captain Cox continues, "All right, so this here company of wagons will hereafter be called The Cox Company."

"Shouldn't we vote on that?" a tall Scandinavian-looking blond fellow asks.

"You want another name, find another company," Cox snaps.

"Just asking …."

"I thought I said not to talk 'less I call on you."

"You did," the man says.

"You're Engstrom, right?" Cox asks.

"Yes."

"I'll say it one more time, Engstrom. Don't volunteer your palaver unless I call on you."

Engstrom merely shrugs.

Red McDuff, who's been standing off to the side, walks over face to face with Engstrom and, with a stubby finger in Engstrom's chest, says, so quietly I can barely hear, "a shrug ain't no answer, Engstrom. When Captain Cox speaks, he expects an answer. Understand?"

"Perfectly," Engstrom says. But he has arms folded and brow furrowed.

McDuff spins on his heel and returns to his spot off to the side.

"Now listen up," Cox begins. "You're to have your weapons charged at all times and near at hand. We'll be coming to the Blue River tomorrow. You all were instructed to have two hundred feet of three-quarter-inch hemp line. You'll use it to help each other cross the river."

Just as he says it, the rumble of distant thunder is heard, and he looks over his shoulder. "Could be the river will rise tonight and the crossing could be a mite tough. Not so tough as the mile-wide Platte can be, but good practice for y'all."

Cox digs a pocket watch out and studies the face. "Camp closes down at 9:00 p.m. We'll rise with the sun and be crossing this little creek by 9:00 in the morning."

A nice fella I'd just said howdy to before the meeting, Johan Engstrom, has his arm raised like he's asking for permission to go to the privy.

"What?" Cox asks.

"I'm still thinking we'd like to vote on the name …."

"And I'm still thinking if you don't like how this company is run, go find another."

"But …."

"Ain't no butts about it, square head."

"I am from Norway. I am no Dutchman."

"I don't give possum piss where you're from. You open

your yap again and you'll be hunting another train—or your teeth—or both."

Standing close behind, his wife Else, equally blond and very pretty, lays a hand on his shoulder, "please, Johan, be careful."

"Yes, papa," a young girl behind her entreats. A very pretty young girl I just noticed for the first time. A very, very pretty girl, and about my fourteen years. She has on a sunbonnet like most the ladies, which extends out six inches and hides her face, but I get enough of a glance to know ....

Else turns to the young girl who I presume is their daughter, "Go back to the wagon, Amalie."

"Yes, mama," the girl says, and hurries away.

Amalie. I'll surely remember that name and know I'll see her again.

Cox spits a gob of chaw on the ground, backhands the remnants from his black beard, then suggests, "She's giving you good advice, pilgrim. Meeting's over. Turn off them lanterns by 9:00."

Everyone quickly heads for their wagons.

As I move away, a hard voice rings out behind. "Hey, there! Hey, you, Zane young'un."

I turn back and Horatio Cox moves closer.

"I'm Jacob," I say, then add, "Jake."

"Good job draggin' in them logs. Wood will come dear from now on."

"Yes, sir," I say, then add, "It was me and Sampson."

"He's your man, so you get the credit."

I can't help but repeat what my father told him earlier.

"No, sir. He's his own man, but I'll tell him you said 'good job'."

"Don't bother."

"Yes, sir."

Shep has been wagging his tail, but stops and I can see his lip curl a little.

Cox spins on his heel and strides away, gathering McDuff up beside him as he goes. I notice him saying something to his foreman and shaking his head seeming irritated as he does.

I wonder if there will come a time when folks recognize there are some Nigras who are free men?

Pa beats me back to the wagon. I can tell by the way he strode off from the meeting that he is angry.

When I get back Sampson is greasing the axle on the cart, Ma is cleaning up our supper dishes over at creek side using sand to scrub the pots, Willy is playing with her dolls, and Edna Mae is darning someone's sock. I walk to the back of the wagon and see Pa reclined inside. An unusual sight—Pa reclining. He's dug out one of his books.

"What are you reading, Pa?" I ask.

"*Wordsworth*. One of his early poems. *'She Dwelt Among Untrodden Ways.'* Appropriate, I think for our journey."

I'm silent for a moment, then can't help but suggest, "Them two, Cox and McDuff...."

"Don't worry about them, son. They're hard men and I'd think you'd have to be in their trade. I won't let them ruffle my feathers too much."

"Mr. Engstrom seems to be looking for grief with every breath?"

"We may be glad he is, should it come all our way. It's nice we share disdain for what appears to be overly gruff men. We'll all settle down before long. We're getting to know each other and, when we do, it's likely Captain Cox won't press folks so hard."

"I hope so."

"I found your *Smith's First Book in Geography* and we've got an hour, so how about you climb up here and study a little."

"Yes, sir," I agree, but my mind's not on the subject as I keep getting visions of a big fight between some of the pilgrims in the company and Cox and McDuff. The two of them have already killed one man, claiming self-defense. Maybe on this side of the Missouri you can club a man from behind and claim self-defense, but back home in St. Joseph I'm sure that wouldn't fly.

And they were on the other side of the river in Missouri when they did so. Maybe, with all the trouble between the states, just one little murder don't mean much? I doubt if the dead man's wife thinks that way and wonder if she went to the law to file a complaint?

I hear Ma's voice raised and peek outside the wagon to see her walking back from the creek, carrying a tin pan and the heavy Dutch oven so I fold my book and jump down. She is walking with a purpose and, when I look beyond, see McDuff standing where she'd been working. He is looking saucy, with hands on his hips and a grin showing his brown snags.

Running over, I take the heavy pot from her. "You okay, Ma?"

"Thank you. Just fine, Jake. Nothing for you to worry about."

But it doesn't look that way to me. I give McDuff a glare, but he is far enough away he probably can't see my snarl and likely wouldn't give a hoot if he did.

I get a truly bad feeling about this day and worry on the days to come. I'm glad Pa didn't notice Ma's voice raised and know she'll be saying nothing to Pa no matter what indiscretion McDuff might have voiced. She doesn't want trouble any more than I do.

Ma is in her late-thirties and still has cream skin and a girlish shape. Like a sweet left out in the sun, I'm sure her looks will draw flies—and McDuff is a filthy one.

Then the flash of nearby lightning and the bone-rattling crack of thunder doesn't settle my nerves any. The good result of the rain beginning to pelt the camp is McDuff hurrying away and Ma and the girls climbing into the wagon to get out of the sudden downpour.

I've already slung my canvas under the wagon and tied it off to the axles so it makes a fine hammock and I climb in out of the downpour.

But with the harsh light of the bolts God is throwing our way every few minutes, and the roar of what could have been a thousand cannons following every bolt, sleep doesn't come until that first black cloud has passed.

And it seems I awaken every few minutes the rest of the night.

Still raining, but just more than a gentle pelting, when I

awake to the sky beginning to lighten to the east. I stay put until Pa climbs out of the wagon and Sampson unrolls from his tarp in the cart.

I perch on the edge of my hammock but the wagon is so low I can't sit up. Still I manage to pull my brogans on then clamber out from beneath to find the mud two inches deep and rain still pattering.

"Help me round up the stock," Pa says, but sticks his head in the back of the wagon before we head out. "Mother, we'll have a cold breakfast of beans, jerky and hardtack."

I grab my little whip from the back of the cart, and Pa carries a long walking stick he seems to have taken a shine to. Then I follow to help him sort out our oxen from dozens of others. I can't help but notice the creek is twice the size it was when we turned in for the night, and with this constant rain, growing.

It's to be the first of dozens of crossings we'll make on this trip.

But as Pa has often said, even a thousand-mile journey begins with the first step.

We return to find Sampson with the mules in harness and our chains and traces lined out for the three yokes of oxen.

Pa and I get the stock sorted and are getting the yokes in place when McDuff strides by and yells over at us.

"Get your asses in gear, and I don't mean them mules." That elicits a crooked laugh from him.

Pa straightens, and yells back. "McDuff, I have ladies in this wagon. I believe by the rules of the company—your rules by the way—that there's to be no swearing or drinking."

He stops, turns and rests a hand on the butt of the revolver he wears. "You don't say. I don't see no ladies."

"Inside the wagon, and you know it well."

"Didn't notice. Get 'em hooked up. We got to cross before that creek floats you away."

"Pa," I caution, and I see him clamp his jaw, but he returns to our chore.

The creek, with fast moving water but only up to the hubs, is easily forded. Still, I have to tie the chickens together, leg to leg, and drop them in the wagon so they don't drown. It's something we'll have to do at every crossing.

The Little Big Blue river will be another thing altogether, if the talk is right.

When we line out after we're all across, we are no longer the last wagon and as fate would have it, I see the wagon ahead is the Engstrom family. And the Engstrom daughter, Amalie, is shining pretty walking along. This time she's left her bonnet elsewhere and palomino blond hair she had in a bun now is a long single braid halfway down her back. Like I said, I'm not likely to forget that pretty name to go with a pretty girl who I think is about my age.

When we're underway, and the stock is lined out and moving on their own alongside the ruts, I gig Stubby up beside Amalie and a younger sister and brother, who are trudging along in the rain and deep mud.

When she glances over, I offer, "I'm Jake. Jake Zane."

"Guess you can't help that," she says, then gets an impish grin.

"And wouldn't if I could," I reply, with almost as sassy a tone as hers.

"I'm Amalie and this is Anakin and Birgit."

"Nice to make your acquaintance," I say.

"Should know each other. It's gonna be a long trip. Nice little mule," she says.

"This is Stubby. Would you like to ride awhile?" I ask.

"Wouldn't mind if I did. Will he tolerate me not being astraddle?"

"He tolerates my sisters." I throw a leg over and slip out of the saddle.

She gets a muddy foot in the stirrup and negotiates her way into the saddle, both legs on one side. I lead and walk ahead suddenly extra glad I have a mount as it's not easy slogging through the mud.

We haven't gone two hundred yards when Pa's voice rings out from behind. "Jake, your stock is wandering."

"Yes, sir!" I shout back, then move back and help her down. "Sorry," I say.

"Duty calls," she says, and gives me a look and smile that is thanks enough.

It's gonna be a long trip but suddenly doesn't seem so bad.

7

WHAT I'VE READ OF THIS TRIP—AND PA HAS A DOZEN journals—water is mentioned many, many times. It's either too much or none, and both are a challenge. For a while, until we cross the Platte, it's likely to be too much as began yesterday. A rainstorm gave us a good wash and faces us in the form of the first of many rivers we'll ford. Not easy streams as we've just crossed, but true rivers that our stock will have to swim and wagons will be roped across so they don't drift away with all our possessions.

We've now been on the trail ten days without incident. We've passed three fresh graves and, of course, wonder what befell those poor folks. Only one had a note attached:

Martha Madigan, 12 years old, skirt caught and she be runned over by our heavy wagon. She is in heaven now.

It's sobering for all of us and Ma gives the girls a lecture about climbing on and off the wagon and cart.

I'm happy to say I have no skirt to catch in the spokes.

That said, the ladies do have one advantage on the trail.

There sure as heck are no privies along the way. The ladies enjoy splits in their undies and full skirts and all they must do is squat and spread their skirts wide to do their business while we boys must find a tree trunk to hide behind or, worse, drop our trousers, which means we must wander off into a copse of trees or tall grass—and, thank the good Lord, there's lots of that except where the stock has grazed it off. We do have our chamber pots along for the ladies doing more serious business and they have the cover of the wagon canvas with flaps front and back for privacy.

I don't know enough about lady things to know how all that lady stuff works, but Ma says it will come with time.

What I do know is I'd like to know more, and would like to spend some time with our fellow traveler, Amalie Engstrom. And maybe steal my first kiss.

The Big Blue River runs south to north where in joins the Platt, so I'm told. As we approach, I can easily make out the occasional white oak rising above blackjack oaks and willows lining the river. The crossing is simple with the river wide but never getting above the hubs and our animals barely slowing. Next is the Little Blue, which I'm told we'll have to rope across if it's running high as it's smaller, but deeper than the Big Blue. I'm hoping we'll get no more heavy rain until after that river. Nice light rains that cool us off and fill some water holes are useful, but those that cause streams and rivers to wash us away are harmful. The Platt, if my reading is correct, is a mile wide and knee deep and seldom gets deeper, only wider, even with a downpour. But it's known to be full of quicksand which can swallow stock or man.

I say simple as I'm driving steers and sheep across and am

smiling when I do so successfully, except for the fact our stock has mingled with a dozen other steers on the far side. I'm cutting ours out when a fellow I have yet to meet charges my why on a hammer-headed sorrel horse, yelling at the top of his lungs.

"That's my friend's black cow your taking." He reins up, mad as the proverbial hatter, shaking his fist at me.

Pa and Sampson are a hundred paces ahead, and neither paying notice.

"And you are?" I ask, trying to be as friendly as possible.

"Jerimiah Rathbone. I'm taking my cow."

I have to laugh, even though I'm pretty sure I'm not making a friend. He's at least five years older than me, and forty pounds heavier, so probably not a good enemy to make … but I can't help myself.

"Well, Mr. Rathbone, where I come from cows don't have that little thing hidden in that tuft of fur you see down there. You sure this is your cow?"

I can see him begin to redden. So, I laugh, and add, "Easy mistake as my steer is likely marked just like your cow."

"Are you shaming me, you smarty alec."

"Well, sir, I'd guess you'd be shaming yourself."

"I ought to drag you off that donkey and whip your butt."

"Won't help you find your heifer. I presume you meant heifer, as my steer don't look like no cow. And my steers and sheep are wanderin' so I gotta get back to it."

"You just remember, smart alec, I don't abide no sass from the likes of you."

I reined Stubby away, but leaned back and yelled at him, "An' just what kind of likes do you abide doing sassing?"

"Not you ... not you!" he yells after me as I drive the steer to join the other stock that are following closely behind Sampson's cart, trailing the big wagon. When the black and white steer falls in I rein up beside Sampson, and I guess he's been paying more attention than I thought. He looks over and shrugs his shoulders in a questioning manner.

"Mr. Rathbone back there thought my steer was one of his cows," I say, and can't help but laugh.

Sampson laughs too and shrugs a couple of times in quick succession, as Rathbone gallops on by without looking over. I start to yell at him that I'll help him search for his friend's cow, but think better of it. He seemed downright irritated enough.

We camp near the Little Blue and, for the first time, have to search more than two miles away for firewood and graze, finally finding the limb of an elm, probably blown off during the recent storm. With Sampson riding George bareback and me on Stubby, we are able to lasso the limb and drag it back to camp. In no time, we have enough wood for tonight and the next five fires, the excess slung in canvas carriers under the wagon front and back of the chicken coop.

Supper is rice, boiled ham, hardtack.

While we are eating Pa, to my surprise as I didn't think he'd noticed, asks, "Seemed you got crosswise with that ol' boy on that ugly sorrel?"

"I hope you weren't arguing with him, Jake?" Ma asks before I can answer. "That's McDuff's nephew and the boy seems out of sort most often."

I again have to laugh. "He thought the steer I was chasing was his cow ... not his heifer, but his cow."

Pa chuckles. "He musta just come down off the moon."

"He took umbrage at me trying to gently educate him," I say, with a wide grin.

Pa laughs again and the girls, Sampson, and Ma join in. We've barely stopped laughing when McDuff walks up and stands with hands on his hips.

"What?" Pa asks.

"Young Jeri tolt me your boy was giving him trouble and all Jeri was doing was hunting a cow?"

"You might think protecting your own is trouble," Ma snaps, standing and striding over only five feet from the big man, "but where we come from that's what one does."

"Well, missy, one shouldn't start trouble as around where I come from, we finish it."

Pa steps up and is quickly between them. "Mr. McDuff, my boy was tending his stock when your Jeri, or whatever his name is, rode up and accused him. Maybe you should take some time teaching him a cow from a coyote. Now if you don't mind, we've only a half hour before lights out."

"You all have been trouble since day one. Just know I'm watching y'all."

Pa smiles at him, his hands on his hips, looking to me like he is mocking McDuff, then says, "You know, Mr. McDuff, I'm pleased to have you watch over us. God knows we'll all need watching over on this long trek."

"Humph," McDuff manages, then spins on his heel and stomps away. "Just watch your manners," he yells back over his shoulder. Then he stops and turns back. "We're coming into Pawnee country and them thieving heathens will steal the shoes off'n your feet, not to speak of the stock. We'll be circling the wagons come tomorrow's camp. We'll be starting to put guards on the stock. Two from lights out to midnight, two more till 4:00 a.m., then two more till dawn. Y'all got the duty from midnight till four. Train rules is if'n your caught asleep on duty, you'll hang from the nearest limb. Understand?"

"I presume we alternate with the other men?" Pa asks, and I can see he's wondering if we are being taken advantage of.

"Don't be a damn fool," McDuff growls. "You won't have the duty again for a week."

"Just making sure," Pa says. "And just so you know, nobody calls me a fool."

"And so what if you got the duty every night?" McDuff says, ignoring Pa's reply.

"Then, Mr. McDuff, you'd find out what unfair brings out in the Zanes."

McDuff curls a lip but laughs and turns and continues away.

Pa glances at me. "I'll wake you at midnight."

But Sampson rises, hands his plate to Ma, and walks to Pa shaking his head and pointing to himself. Poking his own chest again and again.

"You want to take Jake's place?"

Sampson nods strongly.

Pa turns to me. "You can drive the cart and let Sampson sleep some tomorrow."

"I can take my own turn guarding," I say, adamantly.

"Maybe after we get on down the trail."

So, I turn to Sampson. "You get some sleep."

8

WE'VE FALLEN INTO A STRICT SCHEDULE. McDUFF BLOWS A bugle at 4:00 a.m. We rise and gather our oxen and mules and begin harnessing while the ladies fix breakfast, usually porridge or Johnny cakes and coffee, or milk if the cows are producing, or buttermilk from past milkings, if not. Buttermilk will keep for days. By 6:30, we've finished the harness, checked the wagons for damage, and the ladies have repacked all bedding and utensils. At 7:30, Cox or McDuff blow the bugle and yell out, "wagon's ho," and we're off. Normally taking up a position no more than a quarter mile behind the train in front of us. Usually another train is about the same distance behind. At least, so far, the Pawnee would have to be mighty brave to raid a train, as there are plenty of well-armed men.

At noon, if a good place, we stop to rest and eat, usually cold food. After an hour, we're back on the trail. At 5:00 p.m., sometimes before and oft times later when graze is near, water at hand, and a fair camp site, we stop, unpack, and cook supper. It's up to Sampson and me to get the stock to water then graze. Usually by 7:00 p.m., the men have gathered in groups with pipes to smoke and lies to tell and the women do chores and clean up. Often the men break out fiddles and mouth harps, and music drifts across the camp. Guards are posted as it grows dark, usually by 8:00 p.m. It's lights out at 9:00 p.m. as 4:00 a.m. comes before you know it.

Late today we should come upon the Little Blue, the first crossing considered a bit of a challenge. The good news is the weather has held, then two or maybe three days to the Platt and a mile wide, but hopefully shallow, crossing. We'll have been twelve days on the trail, making eighteen miles a day average on this easy trail. After the crossing of the Platt, it's another equal distance, about three hundred miles, of fairly easy going, to some real civilization at Fort Laramie. We're told there's a camp sutler with lots of goods and the savages make camp outside with hides and sometimes meat to trade. Then, it's said, the country gets tougher. But that's fine, as we'll be tougher and so will our stock ... God willing.

Three or four times I've been able to ride ahead and join Amalie Engstrom and her brother and sister, Anakin and Birgit, and let them ride awhile. I hope Amalie likes me at least half as much as I like and admire her. She smiles when many would have furrowed brows and downturned mouth. Occasionally, the men talk her into singing as they play and praise her as having the voice of an angel. And smart! She already knows half the words Ma has been teaching us out of Pa's dictionary. I am surprised when I think I have her stumped with crepuscule, and she comes right back with 'dawn and dusk light'. Dang if that wasn't close enough to the light from first dawn to sunrise and sundown to last light. Then crescive, and she says 'growing' and the dictionary says 'increasing'. She's a tough one to stump. Today's word is circumspect and I can't wait to try and stump her with 'watchful on all sides or cautious'. Pa says now that we're in Indian country we must be circumspect.

The heck if it is, as we're approaching the Little Blue, I've just ridden forward to find Amalie sidesaddle on that big ugly sorrel and Jerimiah Rathbone leading her and laughing like a dang fool at everything she says.

She looks back over her shoulder and sees me as I wheel Stubby around and give him the heels. I don't give her a fare-thee-well. Dang if I'm going to share her with a big ugly galoot like Rathbone.

I'll bet he doesn't know with crepuscule means. Dang his ugly stupid hide. I hope he rots in hell. But I think I best be circumspect when it comes to the big ugly lout.

I shouldn't wish rotting in Hell on anyone, as it seems like every mile we pass a grave, sometimes three or four in a group. I read that the Oregon Trail averages more than ten graves per mile for all it's over 2,000 miles. Dang if I'm not beginning to believe. One time, I counted nine marked graves, all marked cholera and was shocked and a little sickened to see them having been buried so shallow that toes peeked up. I wonder if their kin wasn't sick as well, and decent burying too big a task. It scared my poor little sister, Willy, so much she climbed up into the big wagon between Ma and Pa and couldn't be moved. That is until Pa traded seats with Sampson to drive the cart and she quickly chose to ride with Pa. She still hasn't warmed up to Sampson. If you hadn't spent as much time with him as I have, you would think him a scary sort.

Our stock has fallen right into travelling as a group. You'd think our talk of savages had them bunched. At first, I thought we'd never get sheep, cows, and steers to travel in a single herd, and fairly tightly bunched, but dang if they don't now look like they believe themselves all to be the same critter. It makes my life easy.

I ride forward to watch the crossing begin and am impressed with McDuff as he rides the seventy-five-foot-wide river, only having to swim his horse and a pair of mules he's dragging twenty feet or so. He drags a thick line across, pulls a block and some chain from his saddlebag, ties the block off to a thick elm. The elm's obviously seen a thousand loops of line as it's cut deep. He rigs the line to the two mules then gives a yell to the first wagon. The driver, the young man who's newly married and has his young wife seated beside him, whips up his four oxen and they plunge into the river. The current is not swift but moving. On the far side, McDuff has set two mules to pulling, which counts for a lot as when the fairly light honeymooners' rig hits the short stretch of deep water and the oxen have lost their footing, the rear of the wagon begins to drift. But McDuff is whipping the mule team and soon the oxen have regained their footing. In another twenty yards, the wagon is dragged straight and, in another thirty, is following the team up on dry land.

Uneventful, but a forewarning of what's to come. It will be an experience to watch us cross a river both deep and wide. I'm thinking how wise it was of Pa to caulk the wagon and cart as tight as any skiff. They'll surely need to float.

Three horsebackers cross the river behind the first light wagon and I realize only one of them is there to help McDuff. The other two are to help herding, and I'm glad they are as when it's our turn, my charges—cows, steers and sheep —are strung out for near a hundred yards along the far bank. Some are much better swimmers than others, and I'm lucky to not have had a couple of ewes drift out of sight. I decide to talk with Pa about lashing them all together at the next crossing.

One of the herders who crossed early is only a year or so older than I am, and we are becoming friends as I helped him find a mule that had bolted and lost himself near the Big Blue in miles of thick river willows. We spent half a day riding him down and had lots of time to get to know each other. Tristan McGillicutty—he tells me friends call him Twist—is a bean pole, but strong as wang leather and with a keen sense of humor. He rode, alone, all the way from Charleston, South Carolina, to hook up with a train, thinking he would have to pay to join but rather agreed to work for Cox in return for a blanket and board. He confided in me that he'd lied about his age, claiming eighteen when actually only fifteen. But at a head taller than me, nearly as tall as Pa, he easily passed.

Tristan had lost his Ma to smallpox and was alone, waiting for his Pa to return from working a whaling ship, when word came that the *Pelican* went down with all hands. Nothing held him to Charleston, so he set out with a buckskin gelding and twenty dollars in his pocket. He also confided in me, with some pride, that he still had eight dollars.

I'm happy to learn that he agrees that Jerimiah Rathbone

is a pompous ass, but we both agree that we're neither one someone who wants to upbraid the big lout, or worse, try and black his eyes.

I grab a line tied off to our big wagon, plunge into the Little Blue, and Stubby, faithful mule he is, humps across until his hooves don't touch then strokes with me hanging onto the saddle and dragging along until he gains his footing again. McDuff is waiting and grabs the line and ties a hitch to the line with the block and tackle. The big wagon, oxen plunging forward with Ma and Pa in the seat and the girls in the rear is pulled across in good order. There will be crossings, or so I've read, when the oxen will be unharnessed and will have to swim on their own.

When it's the cart's turn, with Sampson driving, McDuff turns to me. "Won't be draggin' that Black across. He be on his own."

"What?" I ask, a little incredulously.

9

"Ain't helpin' no Negra," McDuff growls. "You want him helped, you help him."

I'm a little shocked but then manage, "Then I'll take the block and tackle line across and tie it directly ...."

"No, you won't. Y'all wanna run with the likes of him, don't be looking for us to help."

"Seems my Pa paid for your help," I say, still a little astonished.

"Don't sass me, whelp. I won't be helpin' the likes of him."

"Tell you what ...."

"What?"

"I won't tell my Pa you said all that, as it would rile him something awful."

"And I don't give a pile of road apples what riles him."

"Well, sir, I do. I'm riding back over and I'll be driving the cart over, and you'll be helping me, right?"

He's quiet for a moment, seeming to chew on that. Then he finally nods. "Ride on," he says. And I do.

When I reach the far bank, I rein up beside the cart. "Sampson, I'll drive the cart over."

He eyes me with furrowed brow, so I add, "We might need your muscle to drag us up the far bank, and besides, your weight is a burden the cart don't need."

He looks as if he doubts my explanation, but shrugs and unloads. I hand him Stubby's reins and the line. He ties it off to the trace chain and we're off.

When we reach the far bank, McDuff stands with hands on hips. He doesn't bother to untie the line but merely waits until Sampson dismounts and does so. Sampson knows he's being disdained by McDuff, but ignores him and takes care of the line. Then he comes over to the side of the cart and waves me down.

McDuff strides up behind Sampson as I dismount. "You take orders from this heathen?" he asks, his tone rude and dismissive.

Shep sidles up, nearly touching my leg and growls.

Duffy looks at my pup and curls a lip. "One of these day's I'm gonna shoot that dumb dog of your'n."

"Then you'll have to shoot me," I say, then change the subject. "Mr. Sampson is fine to work with …" I begin, but McDuff guffaws and spits a wad of chaw right on the toe of Sampson's left boot.

Then he gives me a crooked grin, and snaps, "Keep him away from me or I'll have to fill his ugly hide, and maybe yours with …."

Quick as a cat, Sampson spins and grabs McDuff by the throat with a ham-size hand, and by the crotch with the other. McDuff grunts, his arms flailing, legs kicking, as

Sampson picks him up high over his head, then screams as Sampson takes a half dozen strides and heaves him a half dozen more strides out into the stream. Then Sampson stands with hands on his hips as McDuff flops and screams as the current takes him.

"I can't swim, I can't ..." and he goes under, comes up spittin', then goes under again. Shep runs along the bank, barking. I swear he's smiling, and he sure doesn't dive in to the rescue.

Pa has been coming our way and is witness to most of this but now runs and plunges into the stream and, in seconds, is dragging McDuff to the bank.

Sampson merely climbs back into position on the cart and whips up George and Mark and moves ahead of the big wagon.

McDuff is on his back in the mud, coughing and hacking, spitting river water, when Captain Cox comes galloping up. "What the hell happened here?" he snaps at Pa and leaps off his mount.

Pa shrugs. "McDuff lost his footing I guess. He doesn't seem to swim too well."

Pa reaches down and takes McDuff by the hand and drags him to his feet. He's pale as a ghost and shivering. Shep stands very close to Pa, watching every move Duffy makes.

"You okay, Mr. McDuff?" Pa asks.

He hesitantly nods his head, and Cox asks him again. "Duffy, that the way it was?"

McDuff, to my great surprise, nods, then turns and staggers back and picks up the block and tackle line. I guess he's too embarrassed to admit Sampson has heaved him into the river like a sack of spoiled meat.

The thing of it is, there are two wagons still waiting to cross, and I know they saw everything that happened. It won't be long before the whole train knows.

McDuff will be shamed, and I worry what will happen then. Sampson is big and the strongest man I've ever known, but as Colonel Colt has said, his Colt makes all men the same size, or something to that effect.

And Red McDuff seems to be real handy with his .36 caliber Navy Colt.

WE ARE three days without incident until we come upon a deep cut, only twenty-five feet wide, but equal depth and running with a small ten-foot stream at its bottom. Normally a cut like this would be dug out but this one is so deep it would be a massive undertaken. The cut is heavily lined with oak, elm, and some cottonwood, with thick river willows twenty-five yards wide on either side.

This one has a bridge, and the bridge has a heavy gate with two dozen miserable looking Pawnee's guarding it, four of them standing with arms folded, cradling rifles. Two dozen more stand near a clearing, a camp of ten teepees or so some fifty yards upstream.

The train pulls up and Cox rides his mount from wagon to wagon with a message. "I know this place. The Indians demand a dollar a wagon, five pennies for every animal and person. We can move down stream about four miles and cross fairly easy. But it's still a risk as it's a steep and narrow ravine. It's your choice."

Pa shrugs, and asks, "What did the train ahead do?"

"Paid up."

"And you suggest?"

"Pay up. Better than wrecking."

"Then I guess we pay up."

"Good." With that he reins away to the following two wagons. It will be six bits for our animals, thirty cents for us, and two dollars for the wagons. Three dollars and five cents. It seems a terrible price to pay to save eight or ten miles, but it's not for me to say. These dang Indians are getting rich!

We all cross and get a mile on down the road when I realize I've lost my hat. I had it tied behind my saddle and I guess it came loose. I yell to Sampson to let him know I am riding back, and he gives me a wave. Shep starts to follow, but I send him back to the stock.

I gig Stubby into a gallop, watching carefully for my hat, when I round a curve in the trail see it blown off the trail into the trees. I leap from the saddle and lead Stubby over to pick it up. As I am nestling it on my head, I realize I can see through a clearing to the other side of the cut … and there is Cox. He's standing with one of the Indians, laughing and jawing. Then the Indian hands him a leather poke. Cox gives him a hard look, unties the binding, then pours out a handful of coin. He counts it, replaces it, reties it and shakes the Indian's hand.

Moving deeper into the trees, I wait until he passes me at a gallop, then another couple of minutes. I gig Stubby into a fast walk and follow.

We camp that night in a messy garbage-strewn camp, stinking of human and animal waste, with the broad Platt River stretching out beyond us—stretching so wide we can't make out the far bank in the growing darkness. This is the worst camp we've made in the over three weeks since we left Independence, and I hate it. I'll be glad when are on the far north side of the wide river.

I wait until we've taken our supper before I take up the subject of Captain Cox with Pa.

"What's troubling you?" Pa asks as we head out on guard duty together.

"Captain Cox."

"And?"

"And I lost my hat back near that toll bridge the Indians manned."

"And?"

"And when I rode back to get it, I saw Captain Cox talking with one of the Indians … and he took a poke full of gold coin from the man."

"He got paid … got what they call a kickback from the savages."

"What else would he be paid for?"

"Interesting, son. Good eye."

"What are you going to do, Pa?"

"Bide my time. Sometimes the right thing to do is nothing, but thanks to you, we know who we're dealing with and what to expect. Let's keep this to ourselves."

"Yes, sir."

"There will come a time when knowledge is power."

10

WE AWAKE TO SUNDAY MORNING, AND EVEN THOUGH Captain Cox has some complaint, the large majority of the train wants to have Sunday services and not attempt the all-day crossing of the Platt until Monday morning.

He relents with plenty of grousing. One of the men I've yet to hardly more than give a nod turns out to be a pastor in the Lutheran faith. So, we have services, including hymns accompanied by the guitar, fiddle and mouth harps. It is fine as Amalie and her brother and sister perch on a rock right behind me. I'm pleased when she asks me what is wrong as I haven't come forward on the train to invite her to ride since I saw Jerimiah Rathbone giving her both a stupid grin and a ride on his ugly hammer-headed sorrel.

I, of course, answer in a way I hope won't reveal my jealousy. "Just busy."

"I have something to tell you," she says, and I shrug as if not interested.

Then I make an excuse. "Pa saw some deer track this morning and wants me to try and bring in some fresh meat."

"Come to the wagon when you're finished?" she asks. She looks surprisingly serious, so I agree.

"If we get in before supper time I'll come up."

She nods and runs to join her family.

I've asked Twist to ride along and he's happy to get away from McDuff and Cox, who keep him busy even though he has Sunday afternoon off.

As always, Shep wants to go, but I wave him off and back to Sampson.

As we leave camp, Twist asks me, "Your Pa has lots of fresh meat. How come he's sending you out?"

"He doesn't want to butcher a steer or lamb until we absolutely have to. We've got bacon and sausage still, but we've got a long way to go."

"Makes sense. You praise the Lord every day you still got a Pa and Ma."

I glance over at Twist, who's riding at my side. I swear, he looks like he's gonna get wet eyes. "I am blessed. I know that. Sorry you ...." I don't' finish.

He shrugs.

So, I continue. "You know Ma and Pa would take you in faster than a hummingbird if'n you want to quit Cox."

"I signed on, Jake, and I learned one thing from my Pa he made me swear I'd never forget. That's a man always does what he says he's gonna do ... no matter what. Even the smallest thing. You noticed I ain't never late. If I'm late it means I've done broke a leg or been scalped by the savage."

"My Pa's a stickler on that as well. So if'n I don't show up, you come huntin' me and I swear I'll do the same."

"Swear, on my mama's grave," he says, and I reach over and we, eye to eye, shake on it.

I follow the large track of what I presume is a whitetail buck for over a mile with Twist by my side, then the animal cuts up out of the thicket of river willow that was criss-crossed with game trails. I know enough about whitetail to know they don't range for more than a mile or two, so I'm surprised that this one is close to the heavily travelled and heavily hunted, Oregon Trail.

There's a long winding trail leading up and out of the willows over a swale a half mile ahead, and fresh track is leading us that way. I can see open field ahead as the willows thin. I wave Twist away to the south, and I dismount and wait for him to get some distance. Tying Stubby to a willow where he can graze, I do the five silent steps and wait and look, as my Pa has taught me. After fifty paces, five at a time, I can see a set of antlers sticking up above the knee-deep grass and take a position on my butt where I can rest my rifle on my knee and get a steady shot.

As I suspect, Twist is stalking out into the meadow, hoping to crest the rise and see over. The buck hears or winds him, leaps to his feet to look for the foul odor, and I drop the hammer. He's only forty yards or so and leaps at least five feet in the air. For a second, I fear I've shot low, but he runs for the crest and only makes twenty yards before he goes head over heels.

I can hear Twist whoop. I grin widely even with no one to see ... and move forward slowly. I've knocked deer down before then had them leap up and run not to be found again. Pa's chastised me before about taking my time and letting your game die in peace. So, I do. I see Twist approaching and wave him to plop down as well. I give the buck a good ten minutes while I drop to a knee and reload, then move forward slowly.

He's unmoving. I touch his eye gently with my gun barrel and he doesn't flinch, a sure sign he's dead.

Twist trots up and pulls his knife, and I stop him. "First, we thank the good Lord and this fine eight point for giving us this sustenance." Then I bow my head and give thanks.

"Now?" Twist asks, and I nod, grab the buck's back legs and hoist him so Twist can get to work.

As we start back, two quarters of the buck hanging over the rumps of our mounts and our saddlebags full of backstrap and tenderloins, heart, and liver, we spot a couple of decent limbs some high wind has blown off an elm. We rope them up and drag for camp.

It's near dark when we make it back to the train and to the smiles and congratulations of Ma and Pa, we turn the meat over to them, and Twist is invited to Sunday supper.

While it's cooking, I excuse myself and ride to the Engstrom wagon near the front of the train. Amalie sees me coming and walks my way. Shep is at my heels, and she reaches down and gives his ears a scratch.

"How was the hunt?" she asks, but I see she doesn't wear her normal smile.

"Fruitful. Nice buck. What's up with y'all?"

She glances back as if to make sure no one is in earshot,

then moves closer and rests a hand on my knee as I'm still mounted.

"I overheard something you should know…."

"Okay, what?"

"Jerimiah was talking with McDuff."

"And?"

"And McDuff, if I heard correctly and I may not have … hope I didn't…."

"What, Amalie?"

"McDuff said he was gonna kill your man, Sampson. Maybe this very night."

11

Amalie looks frightened as if she's doing something wrong.

"You sure?" I ask. Seems a long stretch for merely getting dunked in the river. I add, "And Sampson is his own man."

"Whatever. McDuff said he would shoot him down like a dog and no one would give a da ... would care."

I'm silent a moment, chewing on that. Then I nod. "Thank you, Amalie. You're a good soul giving me warning ... giving Sampson warning."

"Don't you tell on me. I don't want that dirty man to have reason ...."

"I won't tell a soul. I gotta get back for supper. Thank you, thank you."

With that I spin Stubby and gig him into a brisk walk back to our wagon. Looks like I have to have a talk with Pa and Sampson after supper. Even sooner if I see Red McDuff headin' our way.

I keep an eye out for McDuff skulking around while I eat

and, immediately upon finishing a plate of salted cod and rice, wave Pa and Sampson over to the cart with the excuse of wanting to show them something. No reason to worry Ma and the girls with this threat ... if Amalie heard correctly.

As Pa and Sampson start to follow me, Twist stands and falls in line. I have to be a little rude. "Twist, this is family business ... sorry."

He looks a little hurt but promptly spins on his heel and strides away.

Once I get Pa and Sampson over to the cart, I carefully relate what I was told. "Maybe we outta be watchful."

"We've got to be watchful every minute," Pa says, and Sampson nods.

"Okay, but especially now. This is what was told me, Duffy was talking to Cox's nephew, Jerimiah, and told him he was gonna shoot Sampson dead."

Pa stares at me a moment, then asks, "Who told you this?"

"I promised I wouldn't say."

"Well, break your promise."

"Pa, in all my days that's the first time you ever told me to break a promise."

He's silent a moment, but doesn't argue with that. "So, is this person credible? Do you believe this or is this informant merely trying to cause trouble?"

"This person has no reason to try to cause trouble, and yes I think her ... this person ... credible."

Pa nods, as if he now knows who reported the conversation to me. Then asks, "And when was this conversation?"

"I didn't ask exactly. But I was asked to come hear the report before I went after the buck this morning."

Pa turns to Sampson, "I want you to make a bed in the cart like it was you. Then take a position out in the brush where you have a clear view of anyone who approaches. Be loaded and ready." Then to me. "You take your regular spot in your hammock under the wagon with your rifle alongside as usual. I'll be on guard in the rear of the big wagon." Then he cautions us both. "Don't be firing at anybody who wanders up. If someone—Duffy—shoots into Sampson's bed, then shoot him down like a dog. Understand?"

We both nod.

I cozy into my hammock and try and stay awake, but I'm tired after spending most the day riding and hunting, then butchering, loading, and dragging the limb back to camp.

So, I'm sleeping hard and jump so hard I tumble out of the hammock when a shot roars out over the camp.

"Where is he?" I hear Pa yell.

"Dunno," I manage, grabbing up my rifle and getting to my feet. Pa jumps from the back of the wagon as Sampson trots up.

"You see him?" Pa asks the big man.

Sampson shakes his head but points off to a spot opposite from where he's been hiding. Pa reaches into the back of the wagon and comes out with an oil lantern, walks to the coals of our cooking fire, gets a twig aflame and lights the lantern, then waves us to follow.

"Show me where," he commands Sampson. We all three are carrying our long arms.

Sampson leads us fifty yards and into the line of brush. Pa

scans the ground and finds some boot prints, seeming fresh, but it's impossible to tell exactly as there are lots of prints from lots of footwear.

Pa shakes his head, seeming disgusted, then leads us back to our wagons. Ma is waiting in her nightgown, her own lantern in hand, as Mr. Engstrom strides up.

"Indians?" he and Ma ask almost in unison. Both Edna Mae and Willy are poking their heads out of the back of the wagon.

"Nope. Some back-shooting coward, I'd guess," Pa says, and walks over to the cart and pulls Sampson's blanket off the pile of goods Sampson has created to look as if he's in bed.

While we're talking, Captain Cox strides up. "What was that shot?" he demands.

"You seen Duffy?" Pa is equally demanding.

"In his bedroll, sawing logs. Why?"

"It's late, we'll come see you, and Duffy, in the morning."

Cox shrugs and stomps away, shaking his head.

Pa watches him go them moves to the cart. "Coward's not a bad shot," Pa exclaims, poking a finger through the fifty-caliber-size hole in Sampson's blanket. Then he hands it to Sampson. "Suggest you make a bed in the brush. In the morning, we'll rearrange our goods so's you're hidden deep in the cart when you're sleeping, after we have a conflab with Cox, Duffy, and that whelp nephew. Now let's get some sleep."

"What went on here?" Ma asks, looking confused.

"We'll talk when we're curled up in the blankets."

AFTER WE'VE GATHERED the stock and harnessed, and while

the ladies are fixing us some fried mush and molasses, Pa waves Sampson and me to follow. He has Sampson's blanket in hand.

Cox and Duffy are working with a teamster on the lead wagon, making a repair on his trace chains when we stride up, all three of us carrying our rifles.

"What?" Cox asks.

I almost smile when I note the surprised look on Duffy's face as Sampson stops only an arm's length from him, giving him a stare that I'm surprised doesn't drive Duffy to his knees. But rather he steps back and has a fist clasping the Colt revolver on his hip.

"Get on with it," Cox demands again.

"Some polecat tried to shoot Mr. Sampson in his bed last night."

"Bullcrap," Cox says. "Likely somebody stumbled and misfired while walking into the brush to do their business."

"Only one man in this camp has a grudge against Sampson," Pa says.

"And who would that be?" Cox asks.

"Sampson threw Duffy here in the river when he showed a threat to my boy, and Duffy damn near drowned. I had to fetch him out. Maybe I shoulda let the current take him away."

Cox turns to his number two, "Duffy?"

"What, boss? I don't need to dry gulch any man. You know I'm good enough to face down any man alive."

"I know you think so. Point is, did you take a shot at Sampson here?"

"Hell no."

"Did Mr. Zane fetch you outta the Little Blue after this man throwed you in?"

Duffy looks embarrassed and glances away.

Cox is more demanding, "Well, did he?"

"I guess," Duffy stammers.

To my surprise, Cox turns on Pa. "I told you this man would be trouble. He risked the life of my man throwing him in the damn river. You get him the hell out of this train. I don't want to see him again or I'm likely to shoot him myself. And I don't miss."

Pa is silent for a count of five, then is equally adamant. "There's nothing in the train rules that says who I can have in my employ. I paid for this trip and you understood we'd be six. You want to refund my two hundred we'll go on our way. Otherwise …."

Engstrom and two others have walked up to see what was up, and all of them joined in. Engstrom, with raised voice, added, "And that goes for me, and Johnson, and Von Richter here. Zane goes, we go too."

Cox clamped his jaw and glared at us for a moment, then in a calm voice, managed, "There is no circumstance you'll get one damn dime of your money back." Then he turned to Duffy. "You stay away from the Zane wagon, you understand."

"Never wanted to have nothing to do with this Negra or anyone who'd have anything to do with him."

"Stay the hell away, understand?"

'No problem," Duffy said, and spun on his heel and stomped away.

"Let's get to the Platt," Cox said, and turned his back on us.

Pa shook hands with Engstrom, Johnson and Von Richter, thanked them, and then said, "Let's get safely across this mile of mud hole," and led Sampson and me back to our rigs.

As we approach the water's edge I'm taken aback by the number of wooden crosses. More graves this side of the Platt than in town cemeteries I've visited. It's not an encouraging sign.

12

THE PLATT LOOKS MORE LIKE AN OCEAN WITH THE TIDE going out than a river. The train in front of us must be half way across and can barely be seen in the mist as we line out and ready ourselves for the crossing.

Captain Cox and Duffy take the lead on horseback with Jerimiah on foot between them, a long pole in hand, testing the depth in front as they move along. The Johnson family, with a huge Conestoga wagon and six yoke of oxen, are in the lead, then the Von Richter's, then two more wagons, then us and our wagon and cart. Engstrom's following us, then a few more, then my friend Twist McGillicutty is riding drag.

We never get water up to the floor boards, but are half way across when I remember the chickens. They've stopped laying days ago, but we were hoping to spread the meat out over the next three weeks. As it is, we have eight drowned chickens when we finally make the crossing after almost six hours of slow going. I apologize to Pa, but he laughs it off and takes half the blame.

I'm totally spent by the time we're on dry ground again as I've had to rope and drag sheep at every deep spot, then gig Stubby, time and time again, downstream to gather sheep and steers. The cows have been tied to the cart, so at least they stay in line. And they only have to keep their noses up, never deep enough to have to swim.

It's only 3:00 p.m. when we gather on the north side of the river, but the men all rise up against Cox and insist on camping and resting up. One family's gimpy crippled steer has downed, and we have eight dead chickens, so we decide to make a celebration of it. There's not enough chicken for all and only about six ounces of beef we'll be able to carve off the young carcass for the six of us, but each family throws in sausage and headcheese or whatever they can.

I've lost respect for Captain Cox, as fairness is a quality my Pa has taught me to respect in a man, and the Captain seems to harbor little. Time will tell.

He's relented to us camping here, but not until he's harangued us for wanting to do so. We passed another half-acre of crosses, must have been four dozen, after leaving the Platt. Again, the sight of them makes my stomach churn. Cox has said this campsite is little more than a sewer, a pisshole he called it, and he may be right.

But we're all exhausted, need to rest, and need a change, and a little celebration may be just the ticket.

Amalie has a half dozen pie pans but not enough dried apples to fill them so comes over to our wagon and asks me,

"Jake, I'm going to make pies for the shindig but don't have enough dried apples. Do you suppose …."

"You've got to ask my Ma. She's in charge of our stores."

"I haven't see her."

"She and the girls are down the river looking for watercress and wild onions to make some salads."

"Which way?"

"Down river. I got to get to plucking chickens."

She laughs. "You'd make a fine wife."

"Ho, ho, ho. Very funny. Down river."

She's still giggling as she walks away. Just as she's heading into the brush, following the muddy river downstream, I see Jerimiah Rathbone on his hammerhead sorrel, and he's watching her. I step back where I'm barely seen next to the big wagon and watch.

He reins up and watches her disappear then, after a few minutes, gigs his horse into the underbrush. He's forty yards farther from the river, but I'm suspicious of what I see.

Sampson is unpacking and rearranging the cart as we have some time on our hands. So, I walk over. "I'm worrying about Ma and the girls. I'm gonna wander down the river aways, keep Shep with you."

He makes a sign like he's plucking feathers then gives me a quizzical look.

"I'll likely have time when I get back." I start for the brush then have second thoughts and turn back. "Hey, if I ain't back in a half hour, you come lookin', okay?"

He gives me a curious look. Then mouths a Duffy?

"No, not Duffy. Just worried about the girls. We are in the wilderness." I flash him a smile but turn and stride off.

And as I feared, I'm only a hundred yards into the brush when I hear a yell, them a muffled scream, and start forward at a trot.

Jeri's horse is tied to a willow branch, and he's got one arm around Amalie's waist and pulling her close with the other hand covering her mouth. She's struggling, but Jeri is big and she's getting nowhere.

I guess he hears me coming and looks back over his shoulder when I'm only two strides away, but he doesn't release her in time and my overhand right gives him a hard whack on his cheek bone. It doesn't knock him down but it does knock him away from Amalie.

He squares away, throws his arms back, then makes the mistake of wiping at the red mark on his cheek. I get another blow to his nose, making him back pedal.

Amalie screams and runs past me. I can see Jeri is not hurt, but he's mad as a crazy man. I'm considering taking Amalie's path and beating a fast retreat, when someone behind me pins my arms at my side. Jeri smiles a crooked smile and in two strides pastes me with a roundhouse right and follows with the left, which I duck. He tries again with a straight right, and I'm able to shove to the side and he misses, but I taste salty blood in my mouth.

Then I hear a solid thump and Duffy drops on his back to the mud beside me like he's had a tree fall on him.

Now Jeri is back pedaling again, wide-eyed and looking fearful. I glance back to see Sampson with his foot in Duffy's chest, then spin back and go after Jeri with new vigor, but he's running for his horse. I grab him by the belt as he tries to mount and drag him back, but he turns and gives me a hard kick. Turning to the side I take it on the thigh, but it makes me stumble back. I can't get to him again before he mounts and gives heels to the sorrel. The big horse kicks mud over me as he digs in and gallops away.

I limp back over to where Sampson stands bearing down with lots of weight on Duffy's chest, and am happy to see that Sampson has Duffy's Colt in hand. Duffy's awake, but wide eyed and holding his left shoulder with his right hand.

He starts to yell at Sampson, "You black bastard …."

But Sampson applies more weight to the boot centered in Duffy's chest, and he screams.

"You're kill … killin'… killin' me," he manages to get out.

Sampson signs with quiet deliberation, pointing down at Duffy then off into the brush, where I see Duffy's horse is ground-tied.

Duffy nods hard enough his thin hair flops back and forth.

So, I add, "Now, you ride on outta here a'fore you make us angry."

Sampson steps aside and Duffy coughs a little as if to catch his breath then tries to turn to his side and stand. But it's obvious his shoulder is injured. He has to turn to the other side to get to his feet. He moves back in the brush to his horse. He has his left arm tucked in close to his side and tries to use his right to grab the saddle horn, but it seems that's not going to work for him. Instead he gathers the reins in hand and takes off at a stumbling walk.

I turn to Sampson. "Thank you, sir. Had you not come along …."

He gives me a tight smile and a grunt.

"What did you hit Duffy with?" I ask.

He spins me so my back's to him and drops a big fist on my shoulder.

I turn back and he puts his fist together then acts as if he's breaking a twig, then points to his collarbone and makes a sound like a crack.

Laughing, I ask, "you broke his collarbone with a whack from your big paw."

He smiles and nods.

"Let's get back to the wagon a'fore he gathers up Cox and tells a bunch of lies."

He nods, and we're off at a brisk walk.

But as we come out of the brush, Captain Cox is already at the wagon, with Duffy and Jerimiah in tow, and Cox has a finger in Pa's chest.

Shep is close to Pa, growling.

13

We walk up the same time as Mr. Engstrom, Johnson and Von Richter, who all stand with hands on hips as they hear Cox out. Four other train menfolk have gathered behind and are watching with critical eye.

"This black bastard ..." Cox says, so angry spittle flies, "... hit Duffy from behind with some damn club and done broke his shoulder. He'll be worthless from here on out. We're gonna hang him."

Before Pa can reply, Engstrom steps forward. It's his index finger poked into Cox's chest, and he's suddenly far more angry than Cox. If fire could fly from a fellow's mouth, nose, and ears, we'd all be scorched.

"You got that near right," Engstrom shouts, "we're gonna hang someone but it ain't gonna be Sampson. Your worthless nephew put his hands on my girl. And we'll hang him here and now or I'll shoot him down like the dog he is."

Duffy who's a half dozen feet behind Cox backs up even farther and rests a hand on the butt of his sidearm. But

Sampson has recovered his Rifle from the cart and has it near leveled on Duffy's middle.

Cox is suddenly dumbfounded, his mouth hangs open as he looks from man to man, hoping for someone to disagree. Then he's angered again.

"That's hogwash, my nephew wouldn't …."

I have to speak up and do. "I saw him, Captain Cox. That's why I challenged him. Then Duffy grabbed my arms from behind so Jerimiah could have at me. That's why Sampson whacked him. And it was with his fist, not with any club."

Cox is silenced again, and turns to his nephew. "That ain't what you tol' me, Jerimiah."

Jerimiah wears a new Navy Colt. He sidles over to Duffy and both of them stand with hands on their weapons.

"Well?" Cox asks. "What the hell …."

Jerimiah has flushed red but then recovers and spits out, "It was her. She came at me like she wanted something and I …."

Engstrom strides forward, fists balled at his side, but Jerimiah draws, cocks and levels his Colt. The blond man stops short. He's heeled, but his revolver is deep in his holster.

Pa grabs the Rifle out of Sampson's hands and cocks it. He level's it on Jerimiah. "Rathbone and Duffy are two guns to ten, if you look around." It suddenly seems Pa is not the only gun at hand, nor the only gun aimed at Red McDuff and Jerimiah Rathbone.

Cox strides forward and knocks Jerimiah's arm up, then grabs his wrist, twists the gun free, and it tumbles into the mud. But he doesn't free the wrist, and Jerimiah stands with a pained grimace.

Then he turns his attention to Duffy. "You got anything to say?"

"All I know is I walked up and this whelp," he motions at me, "was beatin' on Jeri and I put a stop to it by grabbin' him up."

"And," I snap, "letting him have at me while you two cowards ganged up."

Cox holds his hands out, palm out, trying to calm things down. Then, his voice now level, spoke, "All right, all right. We've got a problem here and we'll solve it like we should all problems that don't involve my authority. This day has gone from the promise of a shindig to the need to deal with this young woman's complaints …."

"Complaints hell," Engstrom says, "molestation by your lout of a nephew."

"That's to be decided," Cox says. Then he continues, "I'll appoint a jury of six and we'll get testimony from all involved, then I, as judge, will acquit or pass sentence. Agreed?"

"So long," Engstrom says his voice now more level, "as the sentence is hang the worthless scum by the neck till he's dead."

Now Jerimiah is white as a ghost. He stumbles forward and grabs his uncle by the shoulder and turns him slightly. "You ain't gonna let nobody hang me, are you Uncle Horatio."

Cox growls at him. "Jeri, go put your butt on that log and shut the hell up."

I can see Jeri's lip quiver, but he remains silent and does as ordered.

Cox raises his voice to the crowd. "I'm a fair man," Cox states, emphatically, but the looks on others' faces are not ones of being convinced, "and I'll give a fair sentence if he's found guilty. If y'all know anything about the law in this United States of America, a man is innocent until found guilty. I'll pick the jury …."

"No, sir," Pa snaps, "we'll draw straws out of a hat. No one can claim unfairness that way."

Cox stares at Pa for a few seconds, then with the rest of men shouting, "Draw straws," shrugs and relents. He turns to my Ma, "Mrs. Zane, please use your husband's hat and put twenty-five or so twigs in, the length of your palm, only six of them half the length of the others."

It's the first time I remember Captain Cox ever saying 'please'.

Then he shouts to everyone gathered. "I want all firearms stowed in your wagons. This will be a peaceful trial." And he turns to Duffy. "That goes for you, too, Red."

Duffy doesn't argue, but rather spins on his heel and heads away. I presume to stow his weapon. The other men follow suit, while Ma walks to the nearby shrubs with Pa's hat and completes her assignment:

When all return, Cox yells again, "Y'all line up facing away. You'll draw behind your back. Engstrom won't be drawing, nor will the Zanes or Sampson."

"And why not?" Pa demands.

"Obviously y'all are too close to the dispute."

"There is no dispute," Pa says. "Only a crime to be punished."

"That's yet to be proved." Then he turns to Ma. "Mrs. Zane, please go from man to man. Make sure all they do is reach. No fingering twigs to get a long or short one. No sense going on when you see all six short ones are drawn."

"I'll watch closely," Ma says, and begins.

She gets only halfway through the line when she stops and walks back. "That's the lot of the short ones."

Cox turns to Pa, and snaps, "Zane, you're the prosecutor." Then he eyes the crowd over and points at Van Richter. "Erhard, I've found you to be a reasonable man. A fair man. Can you put up a defense, no matter your feelings on the matter?"

"You bet," he says and nods.

"Then let's have a trial."

14

THE JUDGE, COX, REMAINS STANDING, PUTTING THE ACCUSED, Jerimiah on a log to his left. Then men in the train, not on the six-man jury, numbering thirty or so, drop to their butts in a semi-circle. Erhard Von Richter, the defense attorney, stands at Cox's left on the side of the defendant, halfway between Cox and the men. Pa, the prosecutor, stands on Cox's right. The jury reclines on their butts in front of the semicircle of men. The families, other than two youngsters guarding the stock, crowd behind the semicircle of men, most of them standing.

Cox, very officiously, quiets everyone. "Come to order. Jerimiah Rathbone here is accused of putting his hands …."

Mr. Engstrom, among the seated men, interrupts, "Attempted rape!"

Cox clears his throat. "I'm the judge here and the next man who interrupts me will be banned from camp until this here trial is done. Understand?"

Engstrom says nothing more.

Cox continues, "The prosecution will call its witnesses and the defense with have at them after the prosecution. Then the defense will call its witnesses and the prosecution will have at them. Then the jury will excuse itself and rule. Then the judge will pass sentence if Jerimiah is found guilty."

Then he turned to Pa. "Your witness?"

"I call the victim, Amalie Engstrom."

"Step forward, Miss Engstrom," Cox demands.

"Do I have to," her small voice rings out from the family crowd.

"You do, now," Cox demands.

Her mother, Else, leads her forward and gives her a small push. She moves in front of the jury and stands, her face down hidden by her sunbonnet, hands folded at her back, standing pigeon toed and rocking back and forth nervously.

Cox, in a hard tone, steps forward and instructs her. "Raise your right hand." And she does. "You swear to God above to tell the truth." She nods. Cox steps back.

Pa moves closer to her. "Miss Amalie, this should be very easy. You just relate what happened out in the brush?"

She glances up, then returns to looking at the sod.

"Miss Amalie?"

She begins, but so quietly no one can hear.

"Miss Amalie, you've got to speak up so we can hear you."

"I didn't have enough dried apples to make my pies," she says, then pauses.

"Okay, but out in the brush?" Pa asks.

The volume of her voice raises and I sense she's overcoming her shyness with anger.

"I was hunting your wife ... Mrs. Zane ... to see if she'd

share some dried apples, when Jerimiah rode up and climbed down and strode over. I didn't think a thing of it until he grabbed me by the shoulders and tried to give me a kiss right on the mouth."

She's silent for a moment, so Pa prods her a little. "That's all? He tried to give you a kiss."

"That is not all," she says, volume up another notch. "I tried to bite him, and he yelped. When I tried to push him away, he grabbed my wrist and put my arm behind my back, and then …." She went silent again.

"Then?" Pa prodded again.

"Then … then … then he touched me."

"I'm sorry to be rude, Miss Amalie, but you have to tell us exactly …."

I knew she was so embarrassed that, even angry, she could barely speak, so I spoke up. "Pa, I saw it all."

Cox yelled at me. "Whelp, you keep quiet unless you're called on."

"Yes, sir."

"You finished?" Cox asks Pa.

"Nope," Pa says, then turns back to Amalie. "It seems we have a witness who can describe what might embarrass you. You can give a nod or shake of the head if'n what he says is right or wrong." She agrees with a nod. "So just answer a couple more questions. Were you afraid of Jerimiah?"

She starts to shake her head, then decides she must speak up. "Not at first, but when he … when he tried to have his way with me, I was scared to death and tried to scream, but he put a hand over my mouth." She reaches up and curls her bottom lip down. "He split my lip a little, and when I tasted blood in my mouth, I feared I would faint."

"Have you …" Pa seemed to search for words. "Have you ever given Jerimiah reason to believe he could … as you say … could have his way with you."

Amalie seems to rise up on her toes and bow her neck. Now her tone is adamant and deliberate. "Mr. Zane, I don't know what you think of me, but if you think that I would … that I could …. Well, I'm not that kind of girl. Then I can never speak to you or yours, ever again."

Pa is silent for a moment, then tries to reassure her. "Miss Amalie, I have a job to do here, and that job is to get justice for you and what Jerimiah did …."

Mr. Von Richter speaks up for the first time. "I believe an objection is in order. We have not determined what Mr. Rathbone did or did not do."

"True," Cox agrees, then turns to Pa. "Don't be sayin' he did or didn't did. Understand?"

"Yep," Pa says then turns back to Amalie. "Miss Amalie. Rest assured I believe you to be an honorable young lady." Then he turns to Cox. "I'm finished."

"Mr. Von Richter?" Cox calls on him.

Von Richter walks over in from of Amalie and stares at her for a moment. "You say Jeri put his hand over your mouth. I bet you scared him when you screamed, and he was afraid folks would think just what you've accused him of, even if it wasn't true. Isn't that true?"

Amalie takes a deep breath before she answers. "Mr. Von Richter, all I know is he grabbed me, put a hard hand on my mouth and had just put a hand on me where no man's hand belongs. That's why I screamed."

"I can understand you might have been confused and that frightened you." It wasn't a question and Amalie doesn't reply. So, Von Richter continues, "Miss Amalie, haven't I seen you walking with Jeri and sometimes mounted on that horse of his?"

"I have, right out here in front of everyone and next to my Ma and Pa."

"Has he ever said anything to offend you?"

"He said I was pretty, but I don't see how ...."

"Pretty ... and ... and maybe alluring?"

I can see Amalie clamp her jaw, then almost through her teeth she says, "I believe I know what alluring means, and if you mean I was encouraging him to be forward, you are wrong as a pasture patty in a punch bowl ...."

"Amalie!" her mother yells at her from the family circle.

"Sorry, Ma, but Mr. Von Richter is insulting me."

Von Richter gives Mr. and Mrs. Engstrom a wave and nod, and calls out, "I'm the one who's sorry, Engstroms. This is an impossible job." Then he turns to Cox. "I'm through with this witness."

Then Pa speaks up, "Then I call Jake Zane to be witness."

15

I STRIDE FORWARD AND COX SWEARS ME IN AS HE'D DONE
Amalie.

Pa wastes no time. "What happened?"

"I knew Ma and my sisters were out in the brush hunting
greens, and when I figured they were gone long enough I
went hunting them. I came on Jerimiah here and Amalie. He
tried to kiss her, and she gave a yell and pushed him away. He
grabbed her and put a hand on her, here." I patted my chest
to make sure they understand what I mean, eying the jury
who are nodding.

"When she screamed again, he put a hand over her
mouth. He had another around her waist and dropped it
down and squeezed her here," and I pat my butt.

Again, the jury nods. So, I continue, "So I run forward
and punch him a pretty good one and he lets her go and she
runs."

"And then?" Pa asks.

"We both have our fists up when somebody grabs me from behind and Jeri, being a yellow belly …."

Cox yells at me. "Just tell us what happened. We don't need your opinions of each other."

"Anyway, with my arms being pinned, ol' brave Jeri here gives me a whack or two," I verify what I'm saying by pointing at the knot on my head, then I can't help but laugh before I continue, "but I weren't hurt none. Anyway, suddenly I'm set free and Red McDuff, who was the coward holding me …"—I expect Captain Cox's interruption but it doesn't come so, I continue— "… anyway, suddenly Duffy is on the ground moaning like a lovesick donkey." That gets a laugh out of the crowd. "Then I see that Mr. Sampson over yonder has whacked Duffy a good one and knocked the donkey silly."

I glance over at Pa waiting for his next question, and realize he's gone white, then he sinks to one knee, and I stride over and drop beside him.

"Pa, what's the matter."

"Don't know. My stomach is upside down and my heads swimming."

I yell at Cox. "Pa has to quit this and go to the wagon." Then I turn to Ma and the girls in the crowd. "Take Pa and get him down. Ask Mrs. Albright to come see him." Mrs. Albright is the oldest woman on the train and has already gained the reputation of a healer.

"Sorry," Pa manages to tell Captain Cox as Ma and the girls help him away.

I'm truly enjoying this here trial so I offer my services.

"Captain Cox, if it's right by you I'll take my Pa's position as prosecutor?"

"Won't happen, whelp. You're a witness and you can't be both." He eyes the group of men. "Johnson. Aaron Johnson, will you take over for Zane?"

"Yes," Johnson says and moves forward.

"Then I got to go see to my Pa."

"Not until Mr. Von Richter has had at you."

"Then hurry please."

Erhard Von Richter steps forward. "I understand your concern, Jake. I'll make it short."

"Please," I say.

"You came on Jeri and Amalie after they were already side by side, correct?"

"I guess you could say side by side. He was facing her with an arm around her waist and a hand covering her mouth. She was struggling."

"So, you didn't see the beginning of this affair?"

"No, sir. I said what I saw first."

Jake, so you don't know that Amalie didn't yell and struggle just because she didn't want you to see what was going on."

"I told you what I saw. Can I go now?"

"Run along."

I hear them continue as I run for our wagons.

Mr. Johnson speaks up. "I guess I should call Red McDuff."

Cox looks around, then yells, "Duffy, where are you?" He gets no answer. So, he waves Tristan McGillicutty, his other employee over. "Twist, get on over to our campsite and drag Duffy back here."

"Yes, sir," Twist says, and hurries away.

When I reach the wagon, Ma is standing beside it, talking to Mrs. Albright. She's a buxom gray-haired woman, although there's not much hair on her head. She keeps it covered at all time with a sunbonnet.

"I'm worried," I hear Mrs. Albright say as I hurry up to join them.

"Tell me straight,' Ma says, and I can hear the fear in her voice.

Mrs. Albright takes a deep breath before she begins. "I gave him a pinch on the arm and it was slow to recover. He keeps asking for water, which means he's dehydrated. His eyes are slightly sunken."

Ma has a fist to her mouth and has been biting on a knuckle. She removes it. "I just thought he was tired."

"And the worst sign is his heartbeat. Irregular. That's not good."

"So, what?" Ma asks.

"I hope I'm wrong," Mrs. Albright says, and glances away as if it's hard to meet Ma's eyes.

"Please, ma'am, what's wrong?" I ask.

"Cholera, I'd guess."

"Oh, no," Ma says, and I'm afraid her knees are going to buckle.

If I've seen one cholera grave, I've seen a hundred as we neared and passed the Platt. I ask, "What can we do?"

"Keep him drinking. He's gonna soon have nothing but

water from the backside and dang near nothing in the way of urine. You know I have to report this to Cox."

"I don't care who you tell. I just want my man to get well."

"I wish you the best," Mrs. Albright says, and moves a few steps away. "I feel for you, Margaret, but I won't be coming back and you won't be able to mix with anyone on the train. You are on your own, at least for a few days after ... after Mr. Zane either gets well ... or ... or."

"Thank you, Mrs. Albright," Ma says, and heads for the front of the wagon to go inside.

"Margaret," Mrs. Albright cautions. "I'd advise you to stay distant from Mr. Zane. It seems close contact spreads the sickness."

Ma gives her a sad look. "Could you not help your man were he sick?"

"May God help you all," Mrs. Albright says, and hurries away.

Ma is as adamant as I've ever seen her. "Jake, you stay away from your Pa. Don't even think about sticking your head in." Then she turns to Edna Mae and Willy. "And that goes for you two as well."

"But, Ma, I want to help," Edna Mae says.

"Promise me you'll stay away. All of you, promise me."

And we all do.

"Now," she says, "I've got to take care of your father. Edna Mae, you run the kitchen, Jake, you and Mr. Sampson take care of the wagons and stock. You'll all sleep outside tonight. Where is Mr. Sampson?"

"He was still at the trial when I left," I say. "I suppose he'll have to testify, best he can with a nod or shake of the head."

I can feel the tears well in my eyes but turn away so Ma and the girls don't see. And I see Sampson headed our way.

"What happened?" I ask as he nears. He draws a finger across his throat and I wonder if that means they hanged Jeri from the nearest elm tree, then I see Twist coming our way. I caution Sampson. "Pa may have something bad. Stay clear of the big wagon." Sampson nods and I turn my attention to Twist.

"What happened?" I ask.

"You seen Duffy?" he answers with a question, as he stoops and gives Shep a pat.

"Pa's sick as a poisoned pup and I been doing nothing but worrying about him. I guess we're out of the train until he ... he gets well." I'm afraid to even think of the alternative. I press Twist. "So, what happened with the trial?"

"The jury was out for maybe ten minutes. They found Jeri guilty and Cox banned him from the train. Last I saw he was riding out, his tail between his legs. Don't bother me. You know I think he's lower than a cur dog. It seemed to bother Mr. and Mrs. Engstrom something awful, and Mr. Engstrom yelled at Cox that if Jerimiah showed his face he could expect to get a .50 caliber twixt his ugly eyes. You sure you ain't seen Duffy?"

"So, Duffy is gone too? Maybe he feared he'd get caught up in the hanging business," I have to laugh, but it hurts to even smile with my face knotted up and Pa in a bad way. I get serious. "Twist, you got to stay away for a while till we see what ails Pa, or until the gets well."

"Mrs. Albright was already talking to Cox about y'all and he was warning the rest of the folks when I passed by. I won't come to your wagons, but I'll come within shouting distance and see if y'all need anything."

That almost brings me to tears again. "You're a fine friend, Twist, and I won't forget."

"I'll be back around sundown and check on y'all. Cox told me to tell you ... and I hate to ... that y'all have to harness up and move at least a couple of hundred yards away."

"We got to harness up and move my sick Pa for a lousy couple of hundred yards?" I ask, a little incredulously.

"Sorry, Jake, that's what the captain said. And he said should any of you approach the camp you'll be shot dead."

"Damn him," I say, but nod. And wave Sampson over from messing about his cart.

Now, I guess after moving all we can do is wait.

16

MY PA DIED IN THE NIGHT.

I feel so lost.

Ma has barely spoken, crying and turning away from us. Edna Mae and Willy have not stopped bawling since Ma broke the news to us at daylight. She's already rolled Pa up in his bedding and Sampson is up on a little knoll digging a deep grave.

The idea of putting my father in a hole in the ground and riding away leaves me feeling as if I'm totally empty. I feel like you could drive the big wagon through the hole in my heart.

We're well over two hundred yards from the main crossing and our train is already harnessed up and moving out, and I can see in the distance, over the water, the train following is into the Platt.

Finally, Ma sticks her head out of the wagon and calls Edna Mae and I over. "Edna, you make us some oats and open a new jug of molasses. Jake, harness the cart so we can carry your father up the knoll to where Sampson is digging his grave ..." she pauses and sobs a moment, then continues, "... and we'll have the best service we can. Then we'll eat. We'll stay here until tomorrow and y'all can carve your father a plank to serve as headstone. Then we'll turn around and head ...."

"Pa wouldn't want us to quit," I interrupt.

"You mean we should ...."

"We paid for the train. We'll follow and join up."

"You know, Jake, you are now the man of the family. And you're right, your father would want us to continue. That was the last thing he said to me before he passed."

"Then we go on?" Edna asks.

"We do," Ma says, and clamps her jaw, then continues. "I got a nod out of Sampson earlier. I can drive the cart, Sampson the wagon. By the time we catch up to the train, probably a few days ... presuming none of us takes sick ... they'll take us back in the fold."

I have a catch in my throat, but I clear it and reply, "I'm gonna take a plank off'n the back of the cart and go to carving. What do I say, Ma?"

"Your father was born on February 16, 1812 and he passed last night, May 11, 1851. If you can fit it, he was a good father, husband, and man of God. That should do."

"Yes, ma'am," I say, and head for the cart, first to remove a plank from those separating bedding from the stores below, then to harness up the mules.

By the time I'm finished harnessing, Sampson is walking down the little knoll, leaving a large mound of earth behind, and I presume a six-foot-deep grave.

Edna starts to announce breakfast, but chokes and goes to her knees sobbing, which makes me tear up again and turn away.

Ma climbs out of the wagon, goes to the fire and Dutch oven, serves up a bowl for each of us, and she tops it with a dollop of molasses and a pat of butter. I take one bite, my stomach rolls over, and I'm afraid I'm going to be ill ... then silently pray I'm not getting whatever took Pa. But as soon as I return the bowl to a rock near the fire, walk away and take a ladle of fresh water, I'm fine.

If I'll ever be fine again.

Both Edna Mae and Willy have returned their bowls, Edna Mae having eaten nothing, Willy only a few bites, then Edna turns to Ma. "I want to go home, Ma. Soon as we say words over Pa, I want to go home."

"Me, too," Willy says, with more of a cry that a simple ask.

Ma takes a deep breath, then says in a quiet tone. "Remember, girls, we have no home. We sold the farm ... everything that we don't have with us. Home is where we all are—together."

Willy says, still whining some, "But Pa's not with us. How can we ever have a home ...."

"So long as we're together. Jake is the man of the family now ...."

"But I'm older," Edna Mae says.

"Yes, you are. But Jake is still the man of the family and he'll have Sampson to help us along."

I glance at Sampson, but he's hanging his head, and I believe I see a tear roll down his cheek.

Ma speaks up. "Isn't that right, Mr. Sampson?"

He looks up and his big chest seems to swell, and he nods adamantly.

I hear a shout and look over to see Twist reined up thirty yards away. I walk a few feet closer and yell out to him. "It's the worst, Twist. Keep your distance."

"I saw Sampson diggin' over yonder. Can't begin to tell y'all how sorry I am."

"God's will," I say, but the words sour in my mouth. "We'll be catching up, soon as we know nobody else takes sick."

"I'll be watching for you. And missing y'all till you join back up."

I can feel my eyes wetting up again, and don't try to say anything, but wave and head back to the wagon, where Sampson is dragging the bundle that's Pa out and loading him on the cart. Then he leads the mules up the knoll and the rest of us follow. He takes Pa from the cart and lays him next to the hole then fetches our long manila rope and situates it so he and I can flank the grave and lower Pa to his resting place.

"Wish we had enough planks for a proper box," I mumble.

Sampson gives me a sympathetic look and a tight smile.

Ma responds. "Pa's already in heaven, Jake. Now it's just earth to earth and ashes to ashes. Let's all join hands," she says, and we do. Edna Mae and Willy are sobbing again, and it's a good thing Ma is doing the talking as my throat is closed.

She recites the Lord's Prayer then the verse about walking through the valley of the shadow of death, then reads one of Pa's favorite poems, Wordsworth's *She Dwelt Among Untrodden Ways*, only she substitutes 'he' for 'she'. Then she recites what she wanted me to carve on the plank that I've yet to finish.

When she's done, she turns to the girls. "Go gather up some wildflowers for your father's resting place," then to me, "Please finish your father's marker," then to Sampson. "Mr. Sampson, if you'd be so kind as to cover Mr. Zane. When finished I'd like to break camp and move a mile or so away from where others have camped and soiled the grounds." Then she starts back for the wagons and calls back over her shoulder, "I'm going to start packing. The sooner we can get away from this spot, the better."

As she walks back to the wagons, I hear her sing an old hymn I haven't heard from her in months.

Softly now the light of day
Fades upon my sight away;
Free from care, from labor free,
Lord, I would commune with Thee.
Thou, whose all-pervading eye
Naught escapes, without, within,
Pardon each infirmity,
Open fault, and secret sin.
Soon for me the light of day
Shall forever pass away;
Then, from sin and sorrow free,
Take me, Lord, to dwell with Thee.
Thou who, sinless, yet hast known
All of man's infirmity;

Then, from Thine eternal throne,

Jesus, look with pitying eye.

She doesn't miss a word, and I remember her admonition that I'm now the man of the family. I clamp my jaw and say to myself, man of the family ... man of the family ... man of the family.

So, I head back to my job, carving, saying to myself I must do a job of which Pa would be proud.

Then I begin a new life, without Pa looking over me. Just the thought makes my mouth go dry.

WE SPEND ANOTHER DAY REPACKING, GREASING THE AXLES, and just killing time. The pack of wolves have been worrying us some in the dark, but we've been able to keep a large campfire burning. They've come close enough to worry the stock, to keep Shep with the hair up on his back, and to keep us checking our loads.

On the third morning after Pa passed, Ma calls us together. "It seems the good Lord has spared the rest of us from the cholera. So now we must make time if we're to catch up with the Cox train. We must do so by Fort Laramie. It's been easy going so far, but when we face the Rocky Mountains, it will be a different task and we'll need the help of others. I think we should be on the trail every second of daylight." Then she turns to me. "Do you agree, Mr. Zane?"

It's not the first time I've looked over my shoulder for Pa, but then quickly realize it's me she's asking. "Yes, ma'am. Every second. Dawn to dusk."

"Mr. Sampson?" she asks, and gets an enthusiastic nod.

"How about you, Shep?" she asks the pup with a smile, the first one I've seen since Pa passed. The dog trots to her side and gets a scratch on the ears for his trouble.

"Then," she says, "let's eat, pack and pick up the pace. We'll be going into more interesting country from here on. Columns of sandstone, Courthouse Rock, Jail House Rock, Chimney Rock, Fort Laramie, Independence Rock, and soon the Rockies."

We eat with some enthusiasm and pack quickly.

Ma, now driving the cart, Sampson the big wagon, Edna Mae and Willy walking as they prefer it to the rocking of the wagon and cart, and me on Stubby pushing the stock with the able help of Shep.

We haven't gone a half day and are thinking of eating on the go, jerky and hardtack, when Ma turns the cart over to Edna Mae and climbs in the back of big wagon to dig out our lunch. Then the Indians show up.

The savages ride parallel to us on a ridge to the south. Single file, fifteen of them to my count. Pa had advised me that when the savage rides pulling no travois, no ladies or children among them, the best you can hope for is they are a hunting party. They are a quarter mile from us, so we cannot make out if they are painted up. Pa said that would be a bad sign.

Gigging up beside Sampson I ask, "You see them?"

He nods.

"What do we do?" I ask, and he motions ahead, which I take to mean "just ride on."

I nod, but pull my rifle out of its scabbard and check the load. A single shot cap and ball will do little against fifteen savages if they have mischief on their minds. Before I rein back behind our stock I suggest, "Next chance we get, let's move closer to the main trail and the other wagons."

He nods.

Ma is still in the back of the wagon, so I ride up close enough to call out to her. "Ma, give me Pa's Colt, please. And you take up his rifle and shotgun and make sure our shotguns are ready."

"What's happening," she asks and sticks her head out the back.

I point at the line of savages and she blanches.

I try and reassure her. "No problem yet. But they are keeping pace with us. I've told Sampson to take the first chance to move closer to the other train."

"Good idea. Don't let Shep wander." She speaks as she hands me Pa's Colt in its holster on his full cartridge belt. "I read they eat dogs as handily as we eat chicken."

"Yes, ma'am."

Six cartridges in Pa's Colt, six in mine, six in Sampson's, a load each in our cap and ball rifles, and two loads each in three shotguns. Twenty-seven shots without reloading.

Two of the Indians swing away from the others and rein our way. They keep closing the distance until only a hundred yards from us.

Again, I gig Stubby up next to Sampson. "Make sure they see your rifle and shotgun. I'm gonna try and discourage them."

I give Shep a whistle and he follows at Stubby's heels.

He looks doubtful, but I'm now the man of the family. I rein Stubby away and ride straight for the two Indians.

When I close half the distance I see that, yes, they are painted. I know it means they are going to war, but with whom? We've done nothing to harm them, but we do have things they want. As I near, no more than twenty-five yards from them, they rein up.

So do I. One of them carries an old muzzle loader, both have bows and tomahawks.

I whisper to Stubby. "Stay, Stubby," and circle the horn with his reins, and slowly pull my Colt and Pa's, so I have a six-shooter in each hand. Shep, at my side, begins growling, a low rumble, and the hair on his back is standing.

They say nothing, nor do I. The Indian with the muzzle loader cocks it, but it's not leveled on me. So, I cock both Colts, casually rest one on the saddle horn and let the other hang at my side. My stomach feels as if a ball of snakes is wiggling trying to escape.

The Indians look at each other, and even though nothing is said, both wheel their horses and gallop away, yelling like banshees.

Shep barks as they ride away, but stays close.

I stay quiet until they've rejoined their fellows and I see that all of them are not heading our way, then I un-cock and re-holster the Colts and give Stubby my heels. I take up a position fifty yards short of the wagons, between them and the savages. I have two reasons. The savages should know we mean to protect our wagons and possessions. And I don't want Ma and the girls to see my flushed face. They have no way of knowing how dry my mouth has gone. My stomach is fluttery as a bat cave and as hollow. Soon we cross a small stream, so more than ten or twelve feet wide, and there's a track on its far side, branching off from our rutted trail. As I suggested, Sampson swings the oxen to head toward the train we've been passing. And Ma, who's retaken the cart, follows.

Shep needs little help with the stock: the six steers, two cows, and six sheep. I don't know what we'd do without him.

By turning their way, the nearest train is pulling ahead of us and the next train is at least two miles behind. Even if we make the main ruts, we'll still be isolated with at least a mile from trains ahead and behind.

"Let's pick up the pace," I yell to Sampson and he gives me a wave. His long whip snakes out and cracks over the oxen's heads. Our little herd has wandered away forty yards from our wagons and I give Shep a yell. "Come on, Shep. Move it, move it," and he snaps at the heels of the stock then singles out our most productive milk cow, Patches. Patches is a moody old critter and she tries to kick Shep over the nearby creek. He deftly dodges her kick and give her a nip on the hock. I'm closing the distance to help move the stock along, but am not quick enough. Shep gives the old cow another bark and a nip. She dances forward like a yearling, but steps in a prairie dog hole and I can hear the leg snap from fifty feet distance.

"No," I can't help but shout. She hits the ground on her side, one foreleg broken at the knee and the bottom half pointing off toward Joneses. She's bawling like a wolf has her by the tail. I have no choice but to leap from Stubby and put Patches out of her misery.

We don't have the luxury of leaving her to the wolves, but it would be reckless to stop when the Indians have heard the shot and might approach if for no other reason than curiosity. Seeing a pile of meat that was our cow, might get possessive.

I gig Stubby up next to Sampson. "I got a problem. Can't leave all that meat to go to waste, can't stay here and butcher without watching over my shoulder."

He reaches down into the jockey box the driver rests his feet on, retrieves a line and tosses it to me. He signs tying a knot and dragging her, and reins up the oxen.

When we get close to the main trail and lots of other wagons, and guns, we'll butcher. She'll likely be short of hide on the down side, but it's better than losing three hundred or more pounds of meat.

As I suspect, the Indians, a half dozen of them this time, have closed the distance and are no more than a hundred yards away.

I'm a little surprised when Sampson runs back to give me a hand and is carrying his hunting knife and an ax. In no time he's hacked away a hind quarter. He carries it over to a lone elm growing alongside the creek, and wedges the hindquarter in the crotch of the lowest limb. Even without a tongue, he can make a loud whoop and does so while waving at the Indians.

He points to the hindquarter, then runs back to take his seat in the wagon and whips up the oxen.

Dragging three quarters of Patches behind. When we're no more than two hundred yards from the tree, we see the Indians ride down to investigate, then they give us a wave and I take it as a thank you.

We camp less than one hundred yards from the main trail, and with Ma's grousing to hurry, soon have the cow stripped out and shards of meat hanging on every side of wagon and cart. We'll eat liver and heart our next few meals.

Let's hope we've made friends, at least with this particular group of savages. If what we read is true, they are one of many groups we're likely to encounter.

The next may be less friendly, and we'll likely not have a hindquarter we're willing to give up.

Tomorrow, Ma tells us, we should be in sight of Courthouse and Jailhouse rocks and maybe will camp near them should we run out of daylight.

BECAUSE OF THE WAY WE ARE PUSHING, WE TRAVEL FOR AN
hour after dark—in the crepuscule, which is one of our newly
learned words—as the ruts leave little doubt as to the trail.
We find a trickle of water crossing and flooding the ruts and
turn north for a quarter mile. Ma is reticent—the new word
we learned today—to camp where others have been fouling
the campsites with their mess and their toilet. She's suspicious, since Pa took sick, as it seems many graves are near
filthy campsites. She says it's a suspicious coincidence. So, we
seek sites absent from prior use.

Edna Mae cooks us beef heart and rice for supper, and
her good biscuits. We use the last of our honey and are out of
fresh meat as we're jerking the meat from our old cow, only
sausage, smoked ham, hogback, and dried cod. Ma says, and I
agree since we've seen no game, we're to butcher one ewe
come morning.

We have decent graze close to camp and have not heard a

wolf howl, even so Sampson and I trade off guard duty, and Shep keeps up his faithful shepherding.

I'm up with the sun and am glad I am, as we are less than a mile from Jailhouse and Courthouse Rocks that rise thrusting from the rolling prairie like great medieval castles, not that I've ever seen a medieval castle. But I've seen drawings. The rising sun is washing the huge monuments with gold light, and its shapes and shadows change as the sun climbs.

It's so beautiful I'm reticent—Ma says we should use our new words whenever we can—to soil the earth with blood, but it's eat or die. Selecting the oldest of our ewes, the one most likely to be past bearing another lamb, and lead her, bleating, out into the tall underbrush. I plunge my knife into her heart then as soon as she stills slit her throat. Sampson holds her up by her hind legs and we bleed her out, then skin and quarter her. As fresh meat is dear to us, we take every rib scrap including the rib bones which we'll boil up for Shep. The head we'll roast. Pa had a Mexican hand on the farm for a while, and he taught Ma how to cook *capozelle*, a sheep's head. I've never been able to pop an eye in my mouth—one of the few things I'm sheepish about, to risk a pun.

After we finish I take Sampson by the hand, and as we always do when we slaughter one of our animals, even a chicken, we bow heads and thank the animal and the good Lord for the bounty they've provided. When we're back at the wagons, with the meat rolled in the ewe's wooly hide, we open it and salt down the hide and meat and rewrap. We'll try and tan the hide, coating the inside with a mixture of brains and ash after we scrape it clean, as it will make a fine cloak or some such. I'll need to find a deer to kill to keep us in more meat and brains for tanning.

We're down to buffalo chips for most of our fires as firewood is scarce. We've seen hundreds of buffalo since crossing the Platt. Most of them at a distance, but it niggles the hunter in me as each of those huge critters will provide us with hundreds of pounds of meat, and brains to cure hides.

Willy watches us salt, shaking her head. "I'm not eating old Gretchen," she proclaims adamantly.

I have to laugh. "You named her? Your mistake. Pa taught me long ago we shouldn't name something we might have to eat."

"I saw folks back a ways and they were butchering out an ox. I'll bet they'd named it like we've named ours. And," she says with sudden triumph in her voice, "you butchered poor old Patches."

"And you've been gobbling down jerky from poor old Patches. Shep and you ladies are the only thing Sampson and I won't butcher. Hunger dictates." That makes both Sampson and me laugh heartily. Then I add, "You gotta do what you gotta do."

"Maybe," Willy says, seeming deep in thought. "Still, I don't want to eat Gretchen."

"Sampson and I'll eat your share."

"Humph," she mumbles, and wanders off.

Breakfast of leftover rice with a tablespoon of molasses with a dash of milk, coffee, and biscuits. We pack up and I ask Sampson to rein for the rocks if the country allows. He does and when we're in the shadow of the promontories, I yell to haul up.

"What?" Ma asks, as she pulls rein on the mules.

"Got to mark our passing," I say, and run for a flat vertical sandstone surface with the marks of many others and carve my name and the date. Edna Mae borrows my knife as does Sampson. Willy complains it's too hard for her to do, so I carve out Wilhelmina Zane, and complain to her. "How come Willy wouldn't do. It's lots shorter."

While I'm carving Ma's 'Margaret Zane' in the sandstone, Willy advises me, "Willy is fine for family, but Pa called me Princess and I believe I'll go by that from now on."

"Fine, Princess, but I'm not starting over."

"Wilhelmina is my name, but call me Princess from now on."

"Let's go!" Ma yells from the cart. "We've got catching up to do."

When we're a mile past the rocks, I see a fairly fresh small grave as we near the heavily rutted trail and rein Stubby over to give the marker a read. I'm truly saddened to see it's Amalie Engstrom's little sister, Birgit. The carved plank reads, *Brigit Engstrom 1843-1851 Skirt Caught in Spokes. Run Over. Guard Your Children Carefully.* Mr. Engstrom took some time and care to carve so much on this wide plank.

My sadness is soon replaced by a fire in my gut. We haven't gone another two miles when I spot two riders on a ledge less than a hundred yards from the ruts. They fork horses I recognize, and would recognize their ugly mugs had they not pulled wide-brimmed hats so low. Red McDuff and

Jerimiah Rathbone. Banned from the Cox train, on their own. I'm sure they're living by mischief, likely robbing folks and stealing in the dark of night from one wagon family to sell to another. But maybe I judge too quickly?

I rein up and point them out to Sampson, but can see he's already spotted them. And he doesn't look happy.

But he smiles at me, then makes a gun from his thumb and index finger, aims it their way and says, as clear as he can, "boom."

He smiles at me and I give him a nod, and say, "boom, boom," and he laughs.

We see no more of them through the day, but I'll not rest easy until we're past Fort Laramie in Wyoming Territory. Then we'll likely have far more dangerous challenges.

Ma, who's been acting as our navigator, says it's four or five days to Fort Laramie. It'll be sleeping with one eye open till then.

Then the time to the fort is lengthened. A herd of buffalo is heading north and crossing the trail ahead. We wait at least three hours while two or three thousand animals cross our path. It's the biggest herd we've seen.

We take the time to make a quick camp and cook. Ma wants to eat what we can of the ewe and strip the rest for jerky. Edna Mae makes a rich stew of beans and the last of our carrots and potatoes, so it's a feast.

While we're eating, with buffalo still passing a half mile in the distance, I wonder aloud, "Out of fresh meat. Maybe I should kill one of those big critters."

"Mr. Zane," Ma says, "It would take us a full day to skin

and butcher one of those huge beasts and we have to catch the Cox train by Fort Laramie."

"Just jawing," I say, and go back to my stew.

True to her word, Willy does not touch a bite of Gretchen. Ma fries her a couple of slices of bacon to go with her vegetables and biscuits. Sampson, Edna Mae, and I tease her with lots of "yum yums" as we eat, but she's not impressed.

It's the third night when I'm on guard but dozing in the saddle, when Shep alerts me to full awareness with a burst of growls and barks.

I push Stubby to the far side of our little herd at a trot, counting critters as I go, and realize our two mules are missing.

Back to the wagons at a gallop, I leap from the saddle to see Ma sticking her head out.

"Give me a lantern. Mules are gone astray."

She hands me an oil lantern along with Pa's Colt and gun belt. "Watch out, could be Indians."

Sampson has leapt from his sleeping pad in the cart and follows on foot as I ride back to the herd. I beat him to the far side, dismount and study that perimeter. Sure enough, the tracks of our two big mules lead away. Accompanied by the tracks of two shod horses. Not Indians, if shod.

But Duffy and Jeri are riding shod horses and I'll bet my doubts about them were right.

We can't go on as we have without those mules, and Sampson has nothing to ride without. Which means I'll have to hunt them down alone.

So, it's up to me, now, to ride out and recover our critters.

Sampson signs to me that he'll work on hooking the cart up tandem to the big wagon, but it's an emergency tactic I don't want us to have to take. I must recover our mules.

But I can't track until sunup, and, of course, am so angry I can't sleep either.

19

THE COUNTRY IS ROLLING HILLS WITH FEW TREES, ONLY THOSE lining creek beds. The prairie grass is belly deep when I get far enough from the ruts that I'm past the areas grazed off. It's midmorning, with the sun five times the diameter of the sun over the east horizon, when I see the mules and two horses down a long slope ahead. They're at least a half mile away. I've left Shep with the wagons, fearing that if I catch up with the mules and them who stole them, he'd be barking and give me away should I have to put the sneak on them.

I've been siding to the east of the track of the huge herd of buffalo, but they are out of sight. Still, their trail is well trampled and easily made out as the grass is high on either side of a quarter-mile-wide swath.

I'm pleased to note it's not an Indian village or encampment I'm approaching. The animals are near a creek bed lined with river willows. So, I rein to the west just east of where the buffalo have crossed the creek and travel down the slope to the water-cut-ravine, still a half mile from the critters. I have yet to see any humans but know they must be there.

I dismount and tie Stubby to a willow with enough lead that he can graze and reach water. I pull my muzzle loader and, more importantly, have my own Colt on my hip and Pa's Colt and cartridge belt over my shoulder. Moving quickly in the cover of the ravine and willows, I stay in the shallow creek until I figure I'm less than a hundred yards from my destination. I slip into the willows and stay low.

To my surprise, I'm closer than I estimated. I'm lucky as it seems Duffy and Jeri have not heard me splashing in the little creek.

But they are busy. My mules and their horses are staked out and they are down on their haunches boning out a buffalo calf—and nearly finished with the task. They've done a good job as the skin is spread out flesh side up, covered with a pile of meat that one mule couldn't carry.

I leave my rifle and belly crawl through the grass until I'm no more than ten paces from them and can hear them grouse at each other.

"You're a damn worthless whelp," Duffy snaps.

"Go to hell, Duffy. I done my share," Jeri comes right back at him.

"I shouda' tolt them you said you was gonna have your way with that little Norwegian, and they'd a hung you sure."

I clamber to my feet, a cocked Colt in each hand and both them drop their jaw. "I still may hang your ugly self," I yell out. They both stand and stare.

Their sidearms and rifles are leaned on a rock on the far side of the meat, and I see Jeri eyeing them.

"Don't do it, Jeri," I snap and his shoulders drop.

Duffy gives me a toothy grin. "You ain't gonna shoot nobody," he says. "Hell, you can't get the both of us and you don't wanna die out here in the wild where the coyotes will gnaw your bones."

"You got that part right, Duffy," I say, only I'm not grinning. "Only its likely it'll be your bones on the bill of fare." I've taken a few steps closer so I can't miss if they try something.

Duffy takes a couple of steps away from Jeri, trying to gain my attention I'd guess, then yells at Jeri. "Get your gun!"

And Jeri dives for his weapons.

"Don't," I yell, but he snatches up a revolver and spins my way.

He's not even close to getting the muzzle on his target when the Colt in my right hand barks and leaps in my hand, and he reels back, dropping his revolver and clutching his chest with both hands.

But I'm not going to watch him drop as I turn my attention to Duffy, who takes two steps my way before he realizes my left-hand Colt is dead center in his chest.

"Don't," he says, holding both hands out, palms facing me again, backing away.

Jeri is moaning and frothing, blood billowing on his shirt front, flopping around flat on his back on the ground.

"He's done for," Duffy says, eying me with a little more respect. Then he turns to Jeri and says over his shoulder. "Maybe …."

But I stop him short as going to Jeri is also going to their weapons. "Take another step and you'll join him in Hell."

He stops, again giving me his palms out and backing up.

Jeri coughs a couple of times, sighs deeply, then stills.

I swallow and take a deep breath letting it out slowly. I've killed a man.

Remorse, I should be feeling? Sorrow? But the truth of it is I'm feeling relief. I'm still faced with a dangerous man who's eying me like he'd like to rip my head off.

So, I guess I'll keep him busy. "If'n you want to see another sundown, you'll back off ten paces and plop your butt down on your hands."

He does, and I instruct him, "I'm going to move those weapons away. When I've done so, you're going cut that hide in half, wrap up the good cuts and pack one on each mule. Then you'll suck up the cinch on that sorrel of yours and tie the lead rope of Jeri's paint to the sorrel. Understand?"

He nods, but I can see he's so angry he's red in the face. I stay twenty feet from him, a Colt in each hand, while he works. Luckily both saddles have reatas and he's able to tie off the packs of meat on the mules. Then I have him fill the horses saddlebags with meat.

When he's done, he says, "What now? You can have Jeri's horse, I guess. He won't be needing it."

"That's for a dang sure," I say, then add. "But you ain't telling me what I can or can't do. Now, plop your butt down and pull your boots off."

"What?"

"You heard me. Boots off."

"You ain't gonna leave me out here shoeless?"

"That, or dead. Your choice."

I can see his jaw knot, but he plops down and sucks his boots off.

"Now," I command, "walk on back where you was and lay face down."

He does, and I pick up his boots and fling then over the willows where I hope they've landed in the creek.

"Now," I stay, turning my attention to him. But he has his legs under him and charges off into the grass.

I yell at him. "Keep going until you're atop that knoll. You slow down and I'll be having target practice."

And he runs and runs until he's a hundred yards distant. I shove their muzzle loaders into their saddle scabbards, jam their revolvers into the saddlebags with the meats, and mount up on Duffy's sorrel—now my sorrel.

I know my mules and they follow without lead ropes.

In a half hour, I've gathered up Stubby and lashed his headstall hanging from his saddle and he follows along with the mules.

Before I crest a rise on my way back to our wagons, I turn back to see Duffy heading back to the creek to retrieve his boots. I hope he'll have the decency to at least cover Jeri with rocks so the vultures and critters won't get at him, but I doubt it and don't much give a hoot.

Now, it's join my kin and Sampson, then catch up with the Captain Cox train.

I'd guess I'll be keeping the fact I shot his nephew dead to myself. I have to take a deep breath, let it out slowly and say a silent prayer that thou shalt not kill was meant to read thou shalt not kill except in self-defense.

20

JERIMIAH RATHBONE WAS AS ROTTEN AS THE SOUTH END OF A northbound skunk. Red McDuff may be worse yet, but still I'm remorseful as I lead my string back to the wagons. I can't get the picture out of my mind of Jeri frothing around in the mud and dying hard. It's something I never want to experience again. But should I have to do so with another lowlife, or a savage, I'll do what I must to protect me and mine.

That's something my Pa willed me, and I'll respect the duty.

Sampson, Ma and the girls have not moved the wagons and the ladies run to meet me when I'm only a hundred yards from the camp.

Ma yells out, "Thank God." I dismount and hug them all.

"Isn't that McDuff's sorrel gelding?" Edna Mae asks. "And Jerimiah's paint?"

"Not any more. They gave them up for trying to steal our mules ... forfeited to use one of Ma's dictionary words. They slowed down to butcher a buff calf. Packs and saddlebags are full of meat needs caring for."

Ma looks very worried. "You didn't steal them?"

"Let's say I took them and the meat as reparation. That word you taught us from a few days ago." Then with the girls unloading the meat, I put a finger to my lips and add, "We'll talk on it later," and she reluctantly nods. Then I ask, "Sampson?"

Ma looks a little grave, "He took off after you afoot."

When I get to the pup cart, I unload his mule saddle and cinch up big Mark. Sampson has taken his long arm and Colt but I shove his shotgun in the scabbard and hurry back out to see where I missed him on the return trip. I've gone three miles when I see his big outline on the horizon, trudging away. I pull my Colt and fire a shot and he spins around and is waving both arms. I push the sorrel hard, dragging Mark behind.

He's giving me that toothy grin when I reach him and hand him Mark's lead rope. He gives me a shrug and points at the sorrel.

"Them no goods, Rathbone and McDuff, were the thieves. They made the mistake of killing a buff calf and it slowed them down." I tell him the whole story, with him nodding, as we let the stock set their own pace retracing our tracks.

Before we've gone a mile, I spot some sage hens and dismount and pull his twelve gauge, and in just a few heartbeats have two fat hens in Sampson's saddlebags.

The smell of a big chunk of buffalo roasting reaches us well before we rein up at the wagons.

Ma quickly pulls me aside and I repeat my story.

She looks terribly worried, and sheds a tear or two. "My goodness, Jake. That's a big burden for you to carry."

"Not so much as losing our mules under the circumstance, Ma. Y'all are my responsibility now. The Good Book says as ye sow so shall ye reap. Jerimiah left me with a hard row to hoe, and I had no choice. He went for his gun ...."

Her face hardens and she's adamant. "It is as it is. Let's keep the whole incident, the shooting, from the girls and to ourselves, particularly if we catch up with our train."

"And the sorrel and paint?" I ask. How will we explain having Jeri and Duffy's mounts?

"Set them free or trade them. As much as I know you'd like to hang on to them, they are trouble."

"Yes, ma'am," I say, and decide, tomorrow, to ride back to the following train and see if I can trade or sell them. I've had enough excitement for today.

WE'RE up before the sun as Ma is eager to catch up with Cox, or now, she mentions, join up with another train even though Captain Cox has our fee and we'd likely have to pay another.

Willy cooks some rolled oats, doused in molasses, and we have it and thin buffalo steaks fried up in our big skillet. We're packed and rolling when the sun peeks over the horizon. The train following is camped no more than two miles behind and a mile to the south on the main ruts. Ma chides me before we've gone a mile.

"Jake, I want to be rid of those horses. I can't live through losing another Zane, particularly to a hangman's noose."

"Yes ma'am," I say, and dismount. I drag their saddles and bridles off the pup cart and let the wagons go on while I saddle them and make a pack train from their lead ropes. I backtrack turning southeast where the followers are just coming alive in their camp of fifty wagons.

After a mile or more, I pass a couple of young fellas guarding a herd of dozens of horses, oxen, and meat stock and give them a yell. "Where would I find your train boss-man?"

"Mr. Hogarth. Small wagon with Oregon or bust painted on the cover. Most northerly parked."

"Thanks," I yell and give them a wave. Then I gig Stubby into a brisk walk until I see the painted cover.

Mr. Hogarth, I presume, is already harnessed with a four-up of mules and is dumping his coffeepot grounds when I ride up.

"Mr. Hogarth," I ask.

"I am," he says. He's a smaller-than-average fella with a larger-than-average handlebar mustache. "What can I do for you, young'un?"

"I have two fine horses and rigs to sell or trade. You know of anyone in your train in need?"

He gives me a suspicious look, then walks to the sorrel and paint and gives their legs a rub up and down, as any horse trader would. He eyes me again and asks, "Where'd you come by a couple of fine animals way out here. Saddles, no riders. Suspicious, I'd say."

It sort of gets my hackles up, but I'm in his part of the

world so contain my irritation. "Mr. Hogarth, folks have accidents out here as you well know. These animals are now mine and I need to sell them or trade them. Now there are plenty of trains...."

"Hold your sass, younger. We have some folks might want to barter. Dismount and rest your bones, and I'll be back before you can hum a tune."

I nod and dismount, wrapping Stubby's reins on his wagon wheel, and take up a seat on a log by his buffalo-chip fire.

I'm dozing a little, enjoying the morning sun, when I hear folks coming. I stand, yawn and stretch wide. Then my mouth drops open and I stare. Five men approach, two of them with long arms. They are shouldered and aimed at me.

"Put your hands up, young man!" Hogarth shouts. I hesitate and he yells again, "Now!"

Next to the small train-leader is a sight I'd hoped to never see again. Red McDuff is limping along and glaring at me as if I already had a noose around my neck.

"That's the thieving som' bitch," he shouts.

I stutter, "Me ... me, it's Red McDuff is ... is the no-good thief."

"And he shot my partner dead. Shot him down like he was a coyote."

The others grab me. Before I can explain a whiff, I'm bound with my elbows tied together behind me straining my shoulders something awful.

"He's the damn thief," I manage.

One of the men, a tall fellow with ice blue eyes, white hair and Van Dyke beard, is standing with arms folded.

Hogarth turns to him. "Judge, let's hold up long enough to have a trial and hang this no account."

The man he called judge doesn't say a word, merely smiles and nods. It's the most frightening nod I've ever witnessed.

Am I about to join my Pa?

21

I'm dragged to the center of the circle of wagons and folks gather all around as the judge breaks up some twigs and drops lengths in his hat. Then he goes from man to man asking them to draw, and as soon as he has twelve short lengths he makes those folks gather to one side of a chair he's had delivered. He stands behind the chair with hands rested on the back of it and begins.

"Anyone among you who are not on the empaneled jury know the law?"

A young woman, maybe only a year or two older than me, raises her hand. "I was a clerk for lawyer James LeRoy in Philadelphia."

"A woman," the judge says, rubbing his fingers through his gray Van Dyke. "Sarah, I never ...."

"I can serve as his defense. I know the law."

"Any objections to Sarah Madison serving?" the judge calls out to the crowd, then to the jury. He gets some chuckles but no complaint. My mouth has gone dry and now is even more so as it appears I'm to have a woman, a young woman, as my defense. Dang, if I can't already feel the noose tightening around my throat. I collapse to the sod and cross my legs Indian style.

"Anyone else who can serve as prosecutor?" he yells out.

A man who looks as if he could be a riverboat gambler—waistcoat and four-in-hand tie—strides forward. "I've been on more than one jury, been sued and done some suing myself. I know the ins and outs of the law. At least enough to get this shoat hung and us on down the trail."

"Anyone else," the judge calls out and getting no more volunteers turns to the man. "You'll do, Henderson. Let's get started."

"I object," the young woman who the judge called Sarah says immediately.

"To what?" the judge says. "We haven't even stated the charges yet."

"I'm waiting," she says, and stands with arms folded.

"Murder and thieving," Red McDuff calls out from the crowd.

"Then murder and theft it is," the judge says, with a smile that chills my backbone. He continues, "I'm Judge Lucas Reid, lately of Columbus, Ohio, duly sworn in that state."

"And run out," I overhear a man in the crowd say, and others chuckle.

But the judge is unfazed and continues, turning to my defender. "Now, Miss Madison, you had an objection."

"Habeas corpus, your honor. We have no body, no

evidence of any crime other than this McDuff's claims, and McDuff is a newcomer to all of us ... no one here can speak to Mr. McDuff's character. I suggest we send riders out with Mr. McDuff to the supposed scene of the crime to retrieve the body, if any. McDuff looks to me like a man who'd lie when the truth was better ...."

"Why you," McDuff yells, striding forward until restrained by others.

"I see no reason ..." the judge begins, but then is cut short by the crowd, who shouts their agreement that they need proof of a crime.

A man in a cleric's collar steps out of the jury. "Judge, a young man's life is at stake here. I'll not vote to hang a man unless there's absolute proof of a capital crime."

The judge stares at him a moment, then shrugs. He turns to McDuff. "Can you find this body?"

McDuff sputters. "Hell, you got the horses here. My horse and Jerimiah Rathbone's paint. That's evidence enough to hang this whelp ...."

"Not for me. Your word against his," the cleric says.

"Bullcrap ...."

"That's enough, McDuff," the judge snaps. Then he turns to Hogarth. "Pick two men besides McDuff to ride with you ...."

"We got to keep moving," Hogarth complains.

"We will keep moving and you catch up."

"All right," Hogarth says and points to two others. "First tie this boy and load him in the back of my wagon. I'll need someone to drive my rig," He turns to the crowd.

To my surprise it's my new lawyer, Sarah Madison who

steps forward. "I'll drive and that way I can interview and consult my client on the way."

"Good," the judge says as Hogarth, McDuff, and two others head for riding stock.

I'm happy to say the figurative noose around my neck is loosened, at least for the time being.

"Wagons ho," Hogarth shouts and points west. "See you down the trail," he says as they head for horses. I see them riding out, with a pack mule in tow.

I'm dumped in the back of Hogarth's small wagon. Thank goodness they move my bindings to my wrists in front and to my ankles, then I'm bound to the sideboards. The feeling returns to my forearms and hands and the painful tingling is welcome compared to dead hands.

Stubby is on a lead rope, trudging along behind the wagon.

We barely begin bouncing along the trail when Miss Madison begins interrogating me. By the time we've passed the first two hours, she knows my life story and is well versed on my tale of chasing after my stolen mules, of finding Rathbone and McDuff and the shooting, of me trying to rid myself of their horses, and my reasoning that they are now mine.

She agrees, I'm happy to note.

It's shortly after we've circled the wagons to make night camp, when the four riders return. And the pack mule has a load, which I presume is Jerimiah's body.

I'm starving by the time the rest have had their supper, and Miss Madison comes to the back of the wagon, my jail, with a cup of broth and I'm able to feed myself. She talks as I do.

"The trial will continue in a few minutes. I will call you as a witness and you tell it just as you told me, understand?"

"Easy," I say, "as it's the God's honest truth."

IT'S DARK WHEN WE'RE AGAIN GATHERED, THE JURY TO THE judge's left. The prosecution puts on its case first, which is only McDuff's lies and then showing the horrible remains of Jerimiah Rathbone. Remains that the wolves have been at and are not much more than bones and sinew.

The sight of it turns my stomach and I'm sure has a terrible effect on both the jury and the crowd. Most of whom moan and turn away when the canvass covering Jerimiah is thrown back.

Henderson, the prosecutor, rests his case. Miss Madison begins, first calling McDuff to the stand. He's now cocky.

"That there's your habeas corpse you wanted." He says, and guffaws.

"Do you see a bullet hole in that body?" Miss Madison asks.

"Hell, the critters have had at him. Ain't enough left to put a hole in."

"How do we know, Mr. McDuff, that the critters, as you

put it, didn't kill Mr. Rathbone, or that he was struck by lightning …."

"Ain't no lightning," he growls.

"Hardly the point, Mr. McDuff. Fact is this poor soul could have died of smallpox or cholera or had a heart attack. For all we know he was felled by Indians. Isn't that true?"

"Hell, no it ain't true. That man right there is a murdering back-shooter."

"We'll get to hear from Mr. Zane shortly. Is what I said true or not? No wound that I can see?"

"Well, you can't see so good."

"Can you point out a gunshot wound?"

"Ain't enough left …."

"This witness is excused."

The judge turns to Henderson. "Cross exam, Henderson?"

"Nope," Henderson says, looking smug.

"Then I call Mr. Zane to the stand."

I am sworn on a Bible to tell the truth and do, just as things transpired.

And Henderson is invited to cross examine me.

"So, you admit shooting that poor soul dead?" he asks.

"No."

"No, you just said …."

"I said I shot that lowlife thief who was trying his best to shoot me dead while his fellow thief was going for his gun as well. He ain't no poor soul. I shot that pile of dung in self-defense."

"How old are you, Zane?"

"I'm fifteen in a month."

"Big for your age," he says.

"Grew at least an inch, maybe more, since we left Missouri."

"And you want us to believe you had a gun battle with two adult men and prevailed?"

"If that means I won, yes I prevailed and got my family's mules back. You know dang well they might mean life or death out here in the wilderness. Those two, thieving lowlives were busy when I rode up to retrieve my mules ... stock they stole in the dead of night ... and they decided to make a fight of it."

"And the fact is you shot Mr. Rathbone from where you hid in the weeds. You set out to steal the buffalo calf they'd shot and committed murder in the process. We see no sign of mules and Mr. McDuff says there was no mules, only you, wanting to steal their meat."

"Not how it was," I say.

"That's enough," Judge Reid says, then turns to the jury. "We have a dead man here and two horses the defendant admits belong to the deceased and to Mr. McDuff. I suggest you have a vote and we get on with this hanging."

"I object," Miss Madison screams out. "You're finding Mr. Zane guilty before the jury has had a chance to free him, as should be done ...."

"You're in contempt of this court, Sarah. Now you shut up." Then he turns to the jury. "Y'all get over under that tree and take a vote."

This isn't going well. In only minutes they return. The judge asks, "All right, gentlemen, what's the vote?"

The man with the cleric's collar steps forward. "I'm sorry

to report the vote is seven to five guilty. Seems to me they just want to get on the trail and this boy's life …."

The judge turns to me, interrupting the cleric. "You're to hang from yonder tree until you're dead and cold."

I try but can't speak. The crowd murmurs, some seeming in agreement with my hanging, a few protesting.

"I object," Sarah Madison yells again. "A death verdict has to have a unanimous guilty decision."

"Not in this Oregon Trail court," Judge Reid says, then actually guffaws. Then he waves Hogarth over. "Get him on a horse and under that tall elm. I'm tired and want a drink."

"You're the damn trial boss, Lucas, not the trail boss. You want somebody to hang this boy, you get some volunteers. I'm the one rode my butt raw to get that body …."

The judge ignores him and yells to McDuff, "Get some help and get him on a horse and a rope over that big limb.

Many in the crowd turn and head back to their wagons, but it seems many more are awaiting the spectacle.

I'm dragged to McDuff's sorrel and heaved into the saddle. A man on each side pins my legs to the stirrups as Red, chuckling, leads the animal the forty yards to the elm.

Another man has heaved a manila rope with a noose over a limb. Many of the crowd, including the judge walks along behind.

As they steady me under the tree, I hear hoof beats and look over my shoulder. To my surprise, Edna Mae and Sampson are galloping up on Mark and George and rein to a sliding stop.

"Wait, that's my brother!" Edna Mae screams, and runs

forward. Sampson, too, dismounts and disappears into the crowd.

"Stay out of this!" Judge Reid yells at her. "He's found guilty."

Her eyes flair with panic and she runs to the judge and yells, "He's guilty of nothing. That man," she points at McDuff, "stole our mules and Jake went to get them back."

The cleric steps forward. "New evidence, new trial," he says, adamantly.

While this transpires, the noose is being fitted over my head, even though I'm doing my best to keep it from happening,

"Sampson!" Edna Mae screams, "do something!"

The big man steps from the crowd, behind the judge, and a powerful arm encircles his throat. Reid's a tall man, but not as tall or nearly as massive as Sampson. With his right arm around the judge's neck, and the judge's eyes bulging, Sampson places the point of his large knife just under the judge's jawbone, and gives Edna Mae a nod.

But it doesn't keep McDuff from slapping his sorrel on the butt.

I'm dragged off, airway closed, kicking as if I think I can get purchase in thin air.

Luckily, the cleric is close by and runs and encircles my legs and lifts me, but I'm still choking as the noose has tightened.

As I'm about to black out, I feel the rope go slack then I'm on the ground, someone freeing my neck from the blinding pressure.

When my vision clears, I see I'm not the only one choking, as Sampson still has a death grip on Judge Lucas Reid. As they drag me to my feet, gasping, hands still bound behind me, but breathing and feeling redeemed, I'm shocked again.

Hogarth, the wagon master, has a cocked Colt against the back of Sampson's head and demands. "Let Lucas go or I'll blow your damn head off."

Edna Mae screams at Sampson, "Let him go. Jacob is safe."

For the moment, I think. But, thank God, for the moment.

JUDGE, OR NOW I BELIEVE ONLY SO-CALLED JUDGE, LUCAS Reid, is still trying to catch his breath. Sampson has sheathed his knife and Hogarth's revolver hangs loosely at his side. Edna Mae, my sister and I hope savior, is in Hogarth's face and she's screaming, "You were about to hang my little brother for doing what any lawman would do ... if they had lawmen on the Oregon Trail. And you believed that thief, McDuff, when he should be hanging from that tree." She turns to find McDuff so she can accuse him and searches.

I, too, look the crowd over and realize the sorrel is gone. I listen and can hear hoof beats in the distant. A galloping horse, disappearing into the darkness. Duffy has done what it seems he does best ... run.

"He's gone, run for it," I manage to croak.

Then Edna Mae is right back in Hogarth's face. "Were I a man I'd beat you and him ..." she points at Reid, "... into the ground like the stomped pile of horseshit you both are."

It's the first time I've ever heard my sister swear.

The man in the cleric's collar moves between Edna Mae and Hogarth, and speaks in a low but determined tone. "There has been enough ... enough mistakes made here." Then he turns to Edna Mae. "I suggest you take your brother and your man here ...."

"He's his own man," Edna Mae says, but now in a more reserved tone, sounding like Pa.

"Whatever that may be," the cleric says, "take them and yourself back to your train, and let's forget this ever happened. If that McDuff fellow returns, it will be him on trial."

Edna Mae is silent for a moment, then nods and waves me over. "Let's go find Ma."

But I'm not quite ready. I move over to where Miss Sarah Madison has been watching all this transpire and give her a slight bow. "Ma'am, I'm forever indebted."

She gives me a smile. "Thank God your sister came along. God bless and keep you all."

Then I walk to the cleric and extend my hand and we shake. "Had it not been for you, you'd be reading over me about now."

"God's grace," he says, then adds, "you still want to sell that pinto. Seems your sorrel is under that horse thief, McDuff."

"It's worth fifty and the tack another ten, but if it's you wants him, I'll take a gold eagle for the both."

"I'd be cheating you. How about thirty and we'll call it a deal?"

"I'll give you a bill of sale?"

"I'm fine." He digs in his pocket and comes up with a little purse with a leather throng tie and quickly hands me a ten and a twenty-dollar gold piece.

I make one more stop on my way to fetch Stubby from Hogarth's wagon, and that's in front of the wagon master himself. "Mr. Hogarth, that's the hardest dang sale I ever made. And you almost make a terrible error. I shouldn't give my elders advice, but I'd think you'd want to be more careful in the future."

He nods. "I'll be giving Lucas Reid the boot. He'll be looking for another train on the morrow. You stay well young man." He extends his hand and I shake with him.

"I'll have my weapons and possibles bag back," I say, and he nods quickly and digs my muzzle loader and bag from behind his seat and my Colts out of his wagon box.

Forty minutes later we rein up at our wagons. Ma runs to greet us, and Willy hangs out of the back of the wagon, looking bored.

"What took you so long?" Ma asks, her tone slightly accusing.

"I was just hanging out," I say, and both Sampson and Edna Mae break into laughter.

"What's so funny?" Ma asks, looking confused. Then she reaches over and touches my neck, the red marks, I guess, even visible in the firelight. "Spit it out, what happened?"

WE GET our normal early start, and sometime tomorrow late we should be at Fort Laramie, and then it's into the Rocky Mountains.

We have an uneventful two days, except for Edna Mae

worrying us by waking up sick both mornings. After two days travel we camp on a long gentle slope next to a trickle of a creek that runs to the slowly appearing lights we can see in the distance. Fort Laramie, the last civilization we'll enjoy until we cross South Pass and reach far away Fort Hall on the Snake River.

It would be nice to catch up with Captain Cox and the train, and I hope they are laying over and making repairs at the fort, but only tomorrow can answer that.

Again, just as the sun comes up, Edna Mae, still in her nightshirt, stumbles away from the wagons and throws up into the underbrush.

I'm at the fire with my tin cup extended for coffee, and ask Ma, "What do you suppose is the matter with sis?"

She glances at me, and the anger in her voice surprises, "Nothing for you to worry about. Shouldn't you be hitchin' up?"

"Yes, ma'am, pardon me for worrying about my sis." I try not to be sarcastic with my Ma, but can't help it this time.

She pours my coffee and her voice softens. "It's nothing for you to worry about, Jake. Let's get on to the fort where we can all spend two bits each for a hot bath, and where you and Sampson can work on the wagon without worrying about some savage sneaking up or the stock wandering."

"Yes, ma'am," I say, but I sense the worry in her tone.

Edna Mae returns and dresses in the wagon without taking anything for breakfast. She normally has a good appetite, and that, too, worries me.

Ma is driving the pup cart with Edna Mae beside her; Sampson the big wagon with Willy keeping him company.

Shep and I are driving the stock, when I hear Ma's voice raised.

I don't normally try to poach on other folks' conversations, but let Stubby wander up close to the pup cart, staying just far enough back where I'm not seen for the cover. Ma's raised voice has attracted me. And as I near I can tell Edna Mae is crying, in fact bawling.

"It's terrible to say," Ma's obviously angry, "but I'm glad your Pa didn't see this."

"I'm sorry Ma, I don't know how ...."

"Damned if you don't. When was your last monthly?"

That may be only the second time I've heard Ma swear.

Edna Mae's quiet for a long while, then answers, "Not since we've been on the trail."

"So, likely you're more than two months?"

"All it can be," she says. "It was just that one night."

"Are you sure?"

"Well, pretty sure. One other time, a month before."

I can hear Ma sigh, even over the creaking pup cart wheels. Then say, "God willing, we'll be in Oregon long before the baby comes."

My chin drops. I've been trying to figure out what Ma is angry about, what she wouldn't want Pa to know, and now it's suddenly clear. Dang if Willy wasn't right wanting to bring the cradle. Dang if Edna Mae wasn't right about wanting to stay with that farm boy she had eyes for. More than just eyes, it seems.

24

I'M A LITTLE SURPRISED TO APPROACH THE JUNCTION OF THE Platt and Laramie Rivers and see the fort ahead distantly surrounded on two sides by teepees. There are several groupings of Indian dwellings, and inside them, nearer the fort complex, are at least a hundred wagons. My reading of journals tells me these Indians could be Cheyenne, Sioux, Arapaho, Crow, Assiniboine, Mandan, Hidatsa, or Arikara. Friendly, whomever they may be, or they wouldn't be camped near the fort. Maybe tolerant is a better word than friendly? I presume the wagons, at least some of them, are from the Cox train.

The Platt here is now less than one hundred paces wide and running much faster than farther down river. I presume snow is still feeding the river from the still distant high mountains. As the fort lays south of the Platt, we have to ford. We do, and have an uneventful crossing, although I'm obliged to string the remaining sheep together and drag them across behind Stubby. I then have to move downstream and collect the steers and our remaining milk cow who've been pushed a quarter mile distant. Luckily, all made the crossing.

The fort itself is what's known as an open fort—no high protective walls—a complex of buildings surrounding a parade ground. The plans, of which I've read, originally called for a tall wall enclosing some five hundred by seven hundred feet. That never came about due to its cost and the fact the fort is well protected with troops. Rather, the area is fenced, mostly I imagine to retain stock. As we get within two hundred yards of the gates, I'm surprised to see a rider burst from the buildings and gallop our way.

I can't help but grin when my good friend Tristan 'Twist' McGillicutty pounds up and leaps from his horse. He's laughing as he runs forward and pumps my hand.

"Dang if we didn't think y'all were staked out on an anthill with these damn savages dancing all round y'all and hootin' and hollerin'."

"We've had our share of trouble," I say, "but little from Indians."

"Twist," Ma yells from the pup cart, "Do they have hot water and a tub in that fort?"

"Yes, ma'am. And fat buffalo steaks and taters and the best pies this side of St. Louis."

"You two can jabber later. Let's get inside."

And we do.

The gate guards open the gates wide and we drive right in after I yell to them we need the blacksmith. Not a total exaggeration as we do have a couple of busted fittings. Ma drives right to the sutler and she and Edna Mae dismount. She waves us over and yells to Willy who's with Sampson on the big wagon. Willy runs our way and Ma turns to Twist. "I presume Captain Cox is here?"

"Yes, ma'am. Camped outside with the rest of the train. They've been workin' and repairin' and gettin' ready for the high country."

"Will you please inform him of our arrival and good health, and tell him I'd like to speak with him at his convenience?"

"Yes, ma'am." He, turns and tips his hat to Edna Mae and gives her a big grin, then moves to where he's hitched his horse and rides away.

Then Ma turns to we three young ones, and lowers her voice. "It seems your sister Edna Mae has made a mistake. She's with child."

"How'd that …" Willy starts to ask.

"That's a conversation for another time, Wilhelmina."

"Yes, ma'am. I just was thinkin' you had to be married up."

"Another time, Wilhelmina." Ma's brow is furrowed and her tone no-nonsense. "We'll not speak about this. Not to anyone. Understand?"

Edna Mae is hanging her head, but both Willy and I nod and give her another "yes, ma'am."

"I'm going inside and pick up some supplies and make arrangements for a place to launder our clothes and ourselves. I've been dreaming of a hot bath. You girls come along with me. Jake, please watch the wagons and stock."

She no more than disappears inside when a Dragoon Army officer in full uniform strides up.

"These your rigs?" he asks me, removing and tucking his hat under one arm.

"Yes, sir."

"They can't remain inside. Get them and your stock outside the walls and find yourselves a place to camp."

"Yes, sir, but I'm waiting for our wagon master …."

"Not here, you're not. Don't you see him several times a day?"

"We've been apart from the train. Had some problems with the cholera."

He takes two steps back. "When?" he snaps.

"More than a month ago. Lost our Pa to the sickness. We skipped Fort Kearny because of it and we're in need of the smithy and some supplies. I'll move things out when my Ma returns."

He eyes me up and down. "You're a sassy mouth for a whelp."

I nod and give him a tight smile. "And you're not very welcoming to folks who've been on the trail for months and had more'n their share of trouble."

He smiles a little, then offers, "And you likely got more ahead of you. Keep your stock gathered up and vacate the fort as quickly as you can. Young man, we've had fifty thousand pass through here this past year, and we have strict rules … have to have."

"Yes, sir," I say, and give him a nod. "Thank you."

"We're here to serve," then he laughs. "I wish you were of a mind to enlist. I'd show you trouble."

"Not old enough. And already had my share of trouble, thank you, general."

"From your lips to God's ears," he says, "maybe the next life," and laughs, then adds, "Captain. General is down the calendar a ways."

"I'm sure. Thanks, Captain."

He gives me a curt salute and smiles again. "Out, soon as you can. You're welcome back without the stock and wagons. Riding stock only inside the gates and we barely got room for that."

"Yes, sir."

And he's gone, chuckling as he leaves.

Ma and the girls return, their arms full of packages, and drop them in the rear of the wagon. She has a smile and says, "We ladies are going to the post tonsorial parlor where there is a room set aside for ladies' baths. You and Sampson may come along and use the men's facilities."

"We've got to move the wagons and stock out to a campsite. I suggest we wait outside the gate as a post captain said we can't stay here. When Cox comes along we'll get camped and I'll come back and fetch you."

"And your bath?" she gives me a skeptical look.

"It's warm enough for us to bathe in the river, Ma. I don't want to waste four bits on a little hot water."

She gives me a smile. "You are your father's son. We'll be a while."

"I may be at the blacksmith. If not, I'll perch on the step here."

Laughing, the ladies head across the parade ground to the far side of the post, where a red and white striped post marks the barber and bath house.

Inside the fence reside the fort offices, the sutler, officers and soldiers' quarters, a kitchen and mess hall, a chapel, an armory, the blacksmith and tack shop, and barn and stables all which surround the parade ground. A squad of a dozen Dragoons, Model 1843 Hall rifles on their shoulders, are drilling near the flag pole, and I'm impressed with their coordinated marching as an officer watches and calls orders, with a saber in hand. A tall flag pole with thirty stars and thirteen stripes adorns the center of the parade ground—the thirty first state, California, is yet to be added. Both the offices and quarters are two-story, and, of course, the barn. Four wheeled field cannons are located, each on a limber so its angle of fire is adjustable, each centered on one quadrant of the fence, and each backed with a wheeled caisson with a pyramid of cannon balls stacked on the ground flanking each side.

We leave the pup cart and Sampson drives the wagon while Shep and I gather the stock and we head them outside the fence. I have a little problem holding the stock while we await Cox, as there's not a blade of grass in sight.

It's a half hour before I see Cox headed our way, followed closely by Tristan. Cox reins up and doesn't bother to dismount or extend his hand.

"Took your damn fine time," he snaps, and I'm, as usual, irritated at his mere presence.

25

"WELL, YOU MADE IT THIS FAR," COX CONTINUES, AND I swear he curls his lip.

"We did, in fine fettle, with no trouble we couldn't handle. When are we pulling out?"

"First light. You'll take up the rear."

"Where are we camped?"

"Twist will lead you there. Upstream on the Laramie. We've had some thieving Indian trouble so mind your stock. You'll have to drive them more than a mile to graze so you'd better get with it."

"When it's time. Can't go until Ma and the girls show up."

He shakes his head and curls that lip again. "You're as lippy as your old man was, boy."

I feel the heat crawl up my backbone. Talking about my father is more than I can handle from a man I dislike and have little respect for, a man who employed the likes of Rathbone and McDuff. However, as I killed his nephew, I don't need him riled more than he might be should he find out. I'm pleased to note that Sampson is overhearing our exchange, climbs down from the wagon seat and crosses his arms in front of his massive chest, making his biceps look as big and dangerous as powder kegs.

Even yet, I'm as polite as I can muster. "Mr. Cox, I'd appreciate it if you don't anger me more than my restraint can handle. Don't talk down about my father or I might not be able to control myself."

He chuckles, which heats my backbone even more, then gives me the curled lip again and says, "Your Pa was just fine, sonny. Lippy, but all right. But you ain't him you little pissant, and I don't much give a hoot if you're riled or not. And I don't give a damn if you're there or not when we pull up stakes. We leave first light."

"We'll be there long before," I manage through clinched teeth.

He turns to Twist. "Don't tarry more than you absolutely have to. I got chores for you back at camp," and he whips up his horse and canters away.

I mount Stubby and yell to Sampson. "Going to get the ladies and to the sutler. Anything I can fetch for you?"

He shrugs and I turn to Twist. "I come into a little extra money. How about I buy you a sarsaparilla inside."

We tie our mounts to the sutler's hitching rail and enter the busy place. Soldiers, Argonauts on their way to the gold-fields, and hopeful Oregon and California settlers fill the place.

I buy a bottle for each of us and one for the ladies and Sampson, blowing nearly a dollar to do so, and we park or backsides on the step to sip and watch the Dragoons drill as we drink.

We've cooled our heels for more than an hour when the ladies come striding across the parade ground, and all are smiling. Ma carries a bundle of still-wet ladies' garments and they each wear fresh ones. Even their sunbonnets seem to have a new shine.

The pup cart is awaiting them—I'm a little surprised the Captain hasn't returned and raised hell with me—and all three crowd into its seat, with Twist helping them aboard.

Ma calls me over and asks me to return to the sutler and purchase five more pounds of coffee. She'd hesitated in doing so as it was so expensive, then decided she couldn't face the cold mountains without.

As I wait in line to make my purchase, a burly fellow with a full salt-and-pepper beard, carrying a heavy coach gun that looks to be an eight or ten gauge, is pinning up a wanted poster on a board full of advertisements. Two equally ugly brutes, scared, unshaven, with unruly hair stand behind him kibitzing and each of them is armed to the teeth. As I pass, I study the illustrations. It's a large thing, with seven drawings of wanted men and one comely woman, with the strange name of Madam Matilda. All wanted by slave hunters from Arkansas and Mississippi. A fifty-dollar reward is offered for information leading to the capture of each. And one on the poster is claimed to be a mute. That picture is far too familiar to me—clearly Sampson. The name says *Male Slave Samuel*, but I'd bet my new-found thirty dollars it's Sampson. I wonder why hunters would come this far to capture a slave, then remember that a full-grown male Nigra auctions for as much as three thousand dollars—particularly one with skills as Sampson possesses. For a year's wages, I'd guess hunters would chase them to Hades and back.

I hurry along as I need to get to Sampson and warn him and get him away from the fort. He stands out like a black wolf on the prowl among our white sheep.

I lead the way out the gate, then suck in a deep breath as the guard swings it aside for us, and someone entering.

As I pass through, wagon master Hogarth, mounted on the paint that once belonged to Jerimiah Rathbone, is waiting to enter. He tips his hat and I return the greeting, but continue riding. I hope he doesn't decide to wander up the Laramie River and visit with his fellow wagon master, Captain Horatio Cox. No question the death of Jerimiah and my trial would be an item of conversation—dang, dang, dang. I'm hoping to keep my killing of Captain Cox's nephew unknown to the captain and all on our train. I can't imagine his reaction should he learn the truth.

It's likely he'd at least ban us from the train. And we can't make the crossing of the Rockies on our own. I know there are many spots ahead that will require block and tackle and hundreds of feet of line and many men to move wagons up and down steep slopes.

I'll be walking on eggshells until I hear "wagons ho" in the morning. Both because of Sampson being hunted by some ruthless slave hunters, and the possibility of Captain Cox becoming enraged over my killing his worthless nephew.

It will not be a restful night.

When we get to where Sampson is guarding the wagon and stock, I hurry up beside him. "Trouble." I say, and get his immediate attention. "You're on a poster. Slave hunters from Mississippi are about. You mount up on Stubby here and ride on ahead. We'll join up at the camp."

He nods, looking only slightly worried, but I notice he straps his shotgun scabbard on Stubby, carries his Rifle, and wears his Colt. Stubby gives out a deep grunt as the big man mounts, but he's quickly gone.

Ma shouts to me from the pup cart as he rides away. "Where's Sampson going?"

I'm avoiding telling her about the poster, so don't. "He's been here with all these folks passing by and needs a … a private place off in the bushes."

White lie number one. She nods, but looks doubtful. I whip up the oxen, leave Twist and Shep to drive the stock and lead the way, and we're off to find our camp spot. A distant spot, I hope.

And it takes us more than a half hour to reach the Cox train. We move as far west as we can, upriver beyond the train, taking a spot well past the last of the wagons.

Cox rides out and doesn't bother to say 'hello' or 'go to Hades' to any of us, but rather shouts at Twist. "Damn you, boy. I tolt you to hurry along. It's been two and a half hours."

"Had to wait on the ladies," Twist says, and gives heels to his horse, waving over his shoulder as he passes Cox, who spins his gelding to follow.

We've picked a spot that already has a fire ring, but I see there's no firewood in sight, not even available buffalo chips. And what we try to carry in a sling under wagon is down to only three chips.

At the same time as I notice, Ma gives me a shout, "We'll need something for a fire."

"Yes, ma'am. We'll drive the stock off to find graze and likely return with a load."

"You need Sampson?" she asks.

I don't, but want him away from camp in case some nosy slave hunters come snooping around. "May have to fell a tree," I say, knowing she hates me to risk chopping down trees unless I have company in case of an accident. She nods. I wait for Sampson to saddle Mark and put a pack saddle on George, and we're off, driving the stock in front of us into the low hills south of the Laramie River.

It's funny how Sampson and I have learned to communicate. He has several grunts and I've learned to understand basically what he's trying to communicate. Those and his shakes and nods and facial expressions tell me most of what I need to know. He can read and write, his spelling is not so good, but good enough that if he wants to let me know something he can't communicate without, he can scratch a word in the mud or if Ma has our study materials out, on a pad.

As we ride along, I ask, "Did Pa know you really didn't have your manumission?"

He looks a little sheepish, but then nods. He makes a sign like he's paying out money, and then writing something.

"Someone forged you some papers?" I ask.

He nods, his jaw set.

So, I add, "Pa never could abide with slavery, but I never knew him to lie to Ma about anything. Are we gonna be able to fight shy of them hunters?"

He pats the Colt at his side and the Rifle in its scabbard.

His nod is definite and implicit. There's no question he'll make a fight of it.

I pat my Colt and give him a nod. He shakes his head a little violently and points to his chest, obviously meaning it's not my fight.

"No, sir," I say, equally adamant. "You're family, Sampson. Them old boys come for you and I'd guess Ma and the girls will stand beside me. They ain't taking you back. Ain't gonna happen. That said, I'm not telling Ma about that poster. She's got enough worries."

He looks a little distressed over that and stares off into the hills. And I wonder, is he going to leave us in order to stay out of the grips of the hunters? Or maybe to keep us from being even more involved in his troubles?

"Don't get any ideas, big man," I say. "You signed on for the duration and we need you."

He gives me a weak smile and nods. But I wonder ….

26

It's more than a mile before we find stubble graze in a meadow fed by a little trickle of water, and the trickle above the meadow is lined by some lodgepole pines and chokecherry. In no time I have the pack saddle stuffed with two- and three-inch-diameter firewood, enough for four or five large cook fires.

We move the stock back slowly, letting our mounts and the herd graze as we go. The sun has dropped behind the high mountains to the west as we look down a long slope to our camp. As we near, I rein up and point.

"Sampson, three riders at our fire. You hang back here with the stock until I see what's up."

He nods and I give heels to Stubby and don't slow until I approach the camp.

I relax when I see the three horses are those of Amalie Engstrom, her father Johan and Aaron Johnson.

I'm so happy to see Amalie I embarrass myself with a large grin. Ma has coffee going and I grab a cup and talk too long, then realize I've left Sampson up the slope wondering if he's about to get into a gun battle with a gaggle of slave hunters.

So, I excuse myself and gallop back to where he's still mounted with his Rifle across his thighs.

"Sorry, Sampson. I should have hurried back. It was Mr. Engstrom, Mr. Johnson, and Amalie."

He nods, a little too knowingly and I wonder if it's obvious I like her as much as I do.

By the time we get the stock down to the wagons our visitors are gone and Ma is standing with hands on hips, giving us a bit of a glare. "Did you want me to burn a wagon wheel to cook our supper, or what?"

"No, ma'am," I say, with a bit of a sheepish smile. "We got us a good load."

"Then why didn't you both ride on down here with the wood?"

It's obvious to me she knows something is amiss, but I'm still not ready to fess up to the poster and the possibility of slave hunters roaring into our camp with guns blazing, so I tell my Ma another slight falsehood and hope for the best. "We saw a bunch of sage hens but couldn't get close enough."

I reconcile that as being white lie number two, but still I feel the heat rise on my neck. I don't like lying to my Ma—any kind of lie. But I bite my lip. I'll confess somewhere down the trail and make amends for both prevarications—one of Ma's recent dictionary words—presuming we get down the trail without confronting these black-hearted slave hunters first.

Both Sampson and I sleep restless. My dreams alternate

between walking in a deep grass fresh-green meadow, hand-in-hand with Amalie Engstrom and fighting a bloody battle with slave hunters. Sampson is out of his pup cart at least three times in the night and up with Shep rounding up our stock just as the sky begins to lighten.

We've barely got the pup cart harnessed when I'm surprised by Captain Cox riding up.

"Y'all should begin butchering at least some of your stock as it'll be too dang hard to keep them herded up. You still got five sheep, a cow, and six steers by my count."

"That's right," I reply. "I want to get to Oregon with the beginning of a herd."

"You won't get there with so many and you're better off having them salted or jerked. Way easier to control if'n they're in barrels in your wagon."

"Won't breed in them barrels," I say.

"And won't breed washed away in some river or stole by the Indians."

"True, it's a gamble. But one I'm willing to take."

"Your risk. Y'all run out of meat over yonder don't come beggin'." He's silent for a minute, and I see he's watching Sampson come in leading a pair of oxen, then turns back to me. "That man of your'n, he with you folks long?"

"Since before I was born," I lie, looking him straight in the eye without a blink. "Why do you ask?"

"Had some fellas looking for runaways come to camp last night. One of them runaways was a big ol' Nigra like your man. Big enough to crap on the road and eat a bale of hay."

"He ain't my man. He's his own man," I say, repeating what I've said many times. "My Pa owned his Pa and my grandpa his. Pa kept a promise to his Pa and gave Sampson his freedom. He and his have been part of the Zane family since Methuselah was a pup."

"Humph," he says, then adds, "We ain't pulling out till noontime. Others are using good sense and putting meat up like your wagon master has suggested."

"Good for them," I say, and go back to work.

"Humph," he grunts again, then spins his horse.

I yell after him, "We're likely gonna get a little head start."

He reins up and looks back over his shoulder. "What's the big rush? You remember I said you was to be last?"

"Made some repairs and want to make sure they hold up. When y'all catch up we'll drop to the rear." It's another lie, the part about the repairs, and I wonder if maybe I'm getting too good at the sin. But he merely shrugs, gives heels to his horse and is gone just as Ma calls us to breakfast.

It's time I cautioned Ma and the girls and do so as we eat and as Sampson listens.

"They had a poster up at the sutlers. One of those fellas wanted by slave hunters was big like Sampson. Not near so handsome," I laugh, and hope I'm coming across as casual, then continue. "Just to be cautious and not cause us a delay, I told Captain Cox that Sampson has been with us since before I was born and so was his Pa and grandpa."

Ma is shaking her head, and I know she's not totally buying my sales job, but says nothing until I finish then turns to the girls and surprises me somewhat. "If you're asked, you do as Jake says. Sampson has been with us before any of you were born. Understand?"

Both girls, looking curious, nod, and Sampson gives a

tight grin and a grunt, then goes back to harnessing up the oxen. Like me, Ma seems to value Sampson far more than fear those who might follow and cause trouble. Or maybe my Christian remark sank in?

When finished, Ma sidles up to me. "Jake, I don't think we should get out ahead of the train."

"Ma, I don't want trouble with these slave hunters …."

"And you know Sampson escaped?"

"I know nothing of the kind. He had papers."

"I know he did. Your father said he did. But still you think …."

"Ma, I only think I don't want trouble. We need Sampson and right now I'd guess Sampson needs us. And asides all that, it's the Christian thing to do … keeping him out of Negra hunters clutches even if he had escaped."

She sighs deeply, then nods. "That's for sure. He's got more shackle scars than any man should bare. Let's get on the trail."

"Wagon's ho," I say, and she hugs me. Ma is not given to hugging, so it surprises me a little, but I like it and hug back.

My hope as we whip up the critters is twofold. One, that Hogarth doesn't decide to catch up and visit with Captain Cox and inform him of the death of his nephew; and two, that we're not run down by slave hunters. Cox seemed very interested in Sampson and the poster offered a fifty-dollar reward for information resulting in the capture of a runaway. I'm gaining confidence every day, but the thought of facing the Rocky Mountains and beyond calls on another of Ma's dictionary words—daunting.

CAMPESTRAL, WAS OUR WORD YESTERDAY. OPEN COUNTRY IS what it means, and the campestral will soon be behind us. We'll soon enter the Rocky Mountains in earnest, three hundred miles climbing—ten to fifteen days depending on the terrain—from here to the divide at a place called South Pass. We've been gaining elevation from St. Joseph, Missouri, at just under one thousand feet above sea level, to Fort Laramie at just over six thousand feet above sea level. It's been a gentle rise so far. South Pass and the crown of the continent, as they call the top of the Rocky divide where we'll pass, is just over seven thousand four hundred feet. It doesn't seem like that much more, but it's up and down over broken country and across lots of snow-fed water to get there. And it's a low spot among mountains many of which are in the clouds at over fourteen thousand feet elevation. And those peaks are spectacular … it's seeing the elephant.

From the divide on it's downhill all the way to Oregon. But that too is down, up again, down again, and up even higher more times than all the fingers and toes of all the Zanes and Sampson too.

We left early enough that there is no train in sight ahead of us, and none behind for as far as I can see. To be truthful, during the time we were quarantined—ordered away from the others—I sort of enjoyed travelling alone, except I missed walking with Amalie and riding beside Twist. That said, we had our share of Indian and wolf scares, so group travel is far wiser.

We're not more than two hours on the trail at the end of a long gentle rise when I see dust raised behind us. Only hard-riding horse backers would raise that much dust. I rein Stubby over next to the big wagon now driven by Sampson and yell up to him.

"Hey, big man. Riders coming hard. How about we trade places and you go scout the trail ahead until we know why those fellas are in such a hurry?"

He nods and without pulling the oxen still, jumps from the wagon and takes the reins I hand him. I mount up beside Willy who's riding along with a McGuffey's Reader in hand. She barely notices the exchange. I wish we had time to saddle up one of the big mules as Stubby won't be able to carry him long or quickly, but, right now, all I want is for him to be out of sight.

We're another fifteen minutes, with Stubby and Sampson out of sight up ahead, when I look back to see it's a column of soldiers approaching at a canter. An officer's in the lead, two dozen side-by-side trail him, and a packer and helper follow a quarter mile behind at a jarring trot, each dragging four mules with heavily loaded paniers. The officer lets the others fall in behind the pup cart, reins up beside me and tips his hat. It's the Captain who shooed me and the wagons out of the fort.

"Young man, I'm Captain Haroldson. We met before."

"Yes, sir. You fellas chasing someone? You seem in a big hurry."

"We've a report of some Indian trouble up ahead a few miles. Terrible trouble if it's as reported."

"Dang, I have a scout up ahead, riding alone."

"He's likely to come on the party that were attacked, and possibly upon the savages, which would not go well for him. It's reported to be a small train of six wagons. We understand there are no survivors and most everything is burned to ash. I suggest you turn back until we secure things on the trail."

I'm silent for a second, weighing that, then shake my head. "Can't do that, Captain. But I can hurry us along so we're not far behind you. I can't abandon my friend and scout."

"And he is?"

"Sampson would be his name. You can't miss him. He's riding a little mule and he's dang near as big as his mount."

"Then we'll move on. You see these heathens, you fire three quick shots. It's reported there are more than two dozen of them. Stay on the trail and move quickly. I don't figure this train to be more than three or four miles ahead."

"I'll fire three quick. Thank you."

We've not gone another mile when Sampson comes out of a stand of pine a couple of hundred yards up, south of the trail, but not riding Stubby. Rather, he's leading him. And there's a woman riding a'straddle.

And as they near, I'm surprised to see it's a Black woman. A handsome Black lady who looks mighty like the lady pictured on the runaway slave poster. Madam Matilda, I'd guess.

Ma dismounts from the pup cart leaving Edna Mae at the reins and walks forward as Sampson leads the mule up. I climb down as well.

"Found a lost soul?" I ask, as he stops. I can see the lady is bleeding from scratches on neck and arms, and suggest, "Climb down, ma'am. My Ma will take care of your wounds."

"I'm … I'm Mary," she manages as Sampson lifts her off the mule as if she's a feather.

"Madam Mary?" I ask, and she snaps her head around and looks a little fearful.

"Just Mary," she says, her tone low and suspicious.

"Let Ma take care of you. You're safe here."

"I was with a small train up ahead. We'd just made camp last night and while I still had some light I wandered into the woods for my necessary, when the Indians attacked." With that she breaks down in tears, both hands covering her face.

"Anybody else alive?" Ma asks.

She slowly raises from her face in her palms. "No, mum. I hid and watched and it was horrible. They took two young women with them, they did. As God is my witness there was nothing, not a thing, I could do."

Ma puts an arm around the girl's shoulders and gives her a squeeze. "No one can fault you for living, young Mary. Now let me wash and tend your scratches."

"I ran, fast as I could, through the chokecherries and a patch of wild roses. I was runnin' so scared I hardly knew I was bleeding and all scratched up till the sun rose this morning. May I have some water? I haven't ...." Then she begins sobbing again.

Sampson has moved off and unsaddled Stubby and is turning him out with the stock, so I walk over and join him while the ladies are tending to Mary's wounds.

"Her slave name is Madam Matilda. She was on the poster along with you," I say. He looks up at me and I can see worry in his eyes. "But she's Mary now, if that's who she wants to be."

He gives me a smile and a pat on the back. And he mouths "thank you."

AFTER ASSURING SAMPSON THAT THE LOST LADY HE'S FOUND in the wilderness is welcome to join us, runaway slave or not, I return to the ladies. "Ma, how about you and Miss Mary climb in the back of the wagon and keep doctoring. I don't want to fall too far behind the troops."

And we're soon off. We travel no more than two miles when three dragoons are blocking the trail. One rides forward to meet us.

"You folks need to hold up. Maybe camp right here. We're assigned to guard your camp until our burial detail is complete and evidence collected."

"Any idea what tribe?" I ask.

"Our Sioux scout says Crow or Assiniboine," then he gives me a tight smile, "but hell, it could be Sioux and he's laying it on some other tribe. You don't hardly know ...."

Miss Mary moves forward in the wagon and speaks over my shoulder. "Sir, I was with the Coppersteins and can give some testimony as to what happened."

And I speak up. "If y'all are going to stay with our wagons, my friend and I will go forward and help … help with the burying."

"Are you sure, Jake," Ma cautions from behind me.

"Faster they are done, faster we can pass. But I'm sure it won't be until morning so you might as well make camp." I turn back to the troopers. "I can count on you to stay close?"

"You can," the fellow I presume is of higher rank than the other two reassures me, then adds, "Cap'n Haroldson will want to talk with your maid or whatever she …."

"She's our traveling companion," I say, with some edge to my voice.

"As you say," he corrects, "if she has information he'll add to the report he'll file."

"Then Mr. Sampson and I will take Miss Mary along."

"It's a terrible sight, terrible to see, young man," he cautions.

"She was there so I'd guess it's no worse than what she witnessed."

"How's it happen she wasn't carried off?" he asks.

"She was in the brush when they attacked. She hid out. Dang lucky I'd say."

He nods. "We'll be here until ordered otherwise."

Sampson and I saddle all three mules, with Miss Mary on little Stubby, we start off. I caution Ma, "Remember three shots close if you have any trouble at all. We'll make sure we're back by sundown."

"Stay strong, Jake," Ma says, and I gig George to catch up with the other two.

We haven't gone another mile, winding our way along

the Laramie River, when I smell smoke and see tendrils looping up into the clear blue sky. As we approach, a fine light-gray mare limps by, dragging a broken leg. Two arrows protrude from her side. I hand my reins to Sampson and slip up on her, giving her a reassuring pat on the flanks then withers, then when she stands with head hung, I put the muzzle of my Colt aside her head and put her out of her misery.

When I walk back and recover George's reins, I hear Miss Mary lament, "That was Mr. Willowby's mare."

A pair of dragoons round a curve in the trail pounding our way and pull up next to us. I presume they are responding to the gunshot. I point at the mare. "Put her down," I say and they nod and spin their horses back the way they've come.

We rein up when we're in sight of the skeletons of six wagons and two pup carts. One of them is a huge Conestoga and the others the size of our Peter Schuttler replica, some I imagine from that wagon builder. More than two dozen dead or dying oxen, mules, and horses are scattered around, many with arrows protruding from bellies beginning to bloat. Every kind of household good you can imagine is helter-skelter. Tables, chairs, a fine carved sideboard. A stained-glass window three foot square rests in the mud, one side smashed, what's left showing the image of Mary and baby Jesus—or half the image. There's even an organ burned to its bellows and pump peddles. It makes me wonder if one of those destined to go under-ground is a preacher and organ and stained glass were destined for his new flock. I presume the savages have taken what they could carry and burned what they could not or didn't want.

Up the hillside a hundred feet from the ruts of the trail most the dragoons are digging graves while others are more distant, standing guard. A small remuda of trooper horses are nearby roped in with a portion of the makeshift corral in the river.

Slightly below the graves being dug is a line of canvas covered bodies. More than twenty are lined up, awaiting their everlasting repose. Some are small, even what must be an infant or two.

We rein up a hundred feet short of the smoldering wagons. The distinctive odor of burnt flesh and hair assaults my nostrils.

Captain Haroldson walks over to meet us, and I dismount and extend my hand. "I don't envy your job, Captain. Mr. Sampson and I came to lend a hand."

"Appreciate it, young man, but you best return to your womenfolk. We have plenty of hands here for this heinous work."

So, I suggest, "Before we do, Miss Mary here was with this party. Luckily, she was off in the bushes last evening when the savages attacked. She and your troopers figured you'd want to interview her."

We kill an hour while he interrogates Miss Mary, then we're allowed to return.

And I'm happy to leave. But I can't help but think about the folks in those six wagons and carts. What a terrible way to end more than a thousand miles of hard travel. Stabbed, shot, scalped, life blood soaking the soil of a muddy rutted trail, goods gone or burned. Dreams perished. It's a sight that won't leave me, along with that of Jerimiah Rathbone kicking and moaning and bleeding his last.

I'm thinking of Jerimiah when I approach our wagons and see that the Cox train has caught up with us and, to my surprise, appears to now be well over fifty wagons strong. I presume Hogarth and some of his train have joined up.

And Hogarth has likely advised Captain Cox of the death of his nephew by my hand.

WHEN SAMPSON AND I RETURN TO OUR WAGONS AFTER grazing and watering the stock, I'm not surprised to see Captain Cox having a cup of coffee with Ma and the girls. I am surprised that he doesn't pull his sidearm and start shooting me full of holes.

Miss Mary and Ma are talking and working in unison like two ladies who've known each other all their years. Cox is sipping his coffee and listening to the ladies without comment.

I leap from Stubby and stride over, hoping against all hope that Cox is only passing the time of day with us.

Without bothering with a howdy he gives me a hard look and his voice is low and rumbling a little like the thunder that's been threatening from the west.

"You been at the massacre?" he asks.

"Mr. Sampson and me were there midday and offered to help bury."

"Bad as I'm tolt?"

"Badder than anything I hope to see again. Next savage I see better be headin' the other way and well outta range."

"I understand, but you should understand that they ain't all alike. Just like us, some is good, some is evil … and none of them want us out here."

"I imagine." He's sounding awful easy to talk with and I'm wondering if Hogarth came to visit with him, then he breaks the suspense.

"I had me a long talk with Hogarth, who I understand you done met up with?"

I take a deep breath, and nod. "Wasn't my best visit with folks from another train."

"You want to tell me about Jerimiah and McDuff?"

"Guess I'll have to, although it's been something I've been trying to forget."

It was his turn to say, "I imagine."

So, I go on to relate the whole story of them stealing our mules and me hunting them down. And I tell it just as it was. Miss Mary and Sampson move off and are talking, but Sampson is watching closely, his brow furrowed. I do notice that Ma retires to the big wagon, then see her at the rear just in the shadows of the cover, with Pa's double barrel in hand. It seems she is worried about Cox pulling down on me. But to all our surprise, Cox merely listens, nodding, then when I've finished, he's silent for a moment.

He sighs deeply before he speaks. "I knew that boy would come to a bad end. I shoulda never hired McDuff as he was a poor example for a younger and Jeri took to him. Should he show back up I'll revenge Jerimiah by putting that lousy

Irishman out of his misery. I hope you are telling me the truth?"

"As God is my witness."

"Your tale is supported by Train Master Hogarth, and I have great respect for the man. He's done me a service more than once." The he pauses a moment before beginning again. "Don't surprise me none. Jerimiah and McDuff, I mean. What does surprise me is that a younger like you was able to slip up on McDuff. He's a seasoned trail hand and scout."

"He was busy, like I said. Had his head down busy with butchering and his hands covered with blood and he and Jeri were snappin' at each other like a pair of weasels fighting over a dead hen."

Again, he's quiet, studying me, then he nods. "All right, boy. I'm taking you at your word. It seems you've had the true test. A man with a noose about his neck don't often have reason to lie, that close to meeting the maker."

"I told no lies," I say. Again, I'm surprised as he extends his hand, and we shake.

Then even more surprised when he asks, "I'm short a hand should you want to turn your party over to Mr. Sampson and join up with the Cox Company."

"I'm complimented you think I could do the job, but I best stick with my ladyfolk. My Pa would roll in his grave should I leave before we've reached our goal."

He walks to the back of the wagon and speaks to Ma, "Mrs. Zane, you'll hear no more about this affair from me. You folks keep a sharp eye out. I doubt the savages will try to ravage seventy wagons like they did that six. Suggest you keep the girls busy in the wagon when we pass. A couple of dozen fresh graves and all their goods burned to ash is nothing for them to see."

He heads to his horse, mounts up and waves over his shoulder as he moves away.

I'm still bothered by seeing Captain Cox take money from the Indians all of us paid to cross their bridge and vow to myself to confront him with what I think was a heinous act on his part. But that will come way on down the trail. The fact is, each of us has his frailties. I've lied to my Ma, white lies I think, but lies nonetheless. Captain Cox has taken money, more than the agreed amount for our passing. That said, I'll give him the opportunity to explain.

Ma climbs down and yells at the girls. "Get supper going. Dig out a ham. I've got my appetite back." Then she turns to me. "I'm glad that is behind us."

"Cost me many hours of sleep," I say.

"I hope you can rest easy and only worry about what's ahead of us and forget the past."

I give her a tight grin, but the fact is, I won't rest easy until we're safe in Oregon and off this damnable trail, which both excites and dooms me to worry. But as Pa told me, take it as it comes; face each day, each hour, each minute, and all you can do is your best.

And I think I've learned something about human nature. Captain Cox is a hard man, but I'm surprised, in fact shocked, to learn he's a fair man. He employed McDuff as his number two likely because he had a reputation as a scout, and his own nephew likely because he was family. Neither of them turned out to be worth spit, but he fairly judged them and me. A man is not always what he seems, at times better, at times worse. I'll be slower to judge in the future.

The thunder announces a change in the weather, and I'm not surprised to awaken in the middle of the night to flashes and roars like cannon fire that light the sky and a beating rain. We've been fortunate to have had great weather and hardly more than a sprinkle to date, but if there's one certainty on the Oregon Trail, things will change, and change often. Particularly in the Rocky Mountains if I can believe the journals I've read.

Morning finds us eating warmed over beans and ham for breakfast, and on the trail with the girls and Miss Mary in the big wagon with Sampson at the whip, and Ma driving the pup cart wrapped in a canvas but looking like a drowned cat with hair hanging straight from her sunbonnet. And me in my slicker driving the stock with Shep having to work hard as the stock is head down, unhappy about heading into a driving rain storm. We fall in near the front of the train and I'm pleased there was a space. I expect Captain Cox to come chastise me as he's said we're to take the tail end, but he seems reticent to give me more trouble than I've already had.

The good news is as we pass the six wagons and two dozen graves, the girls are busy with their studies and don't look up and out. Captain Haroldson falls in beside me and paces me for a while. He's talking as rain drips off his cap's eyeshade and pours down his oilskin slicker. He greets Ma before he drops back beside me. I'm a bit taken back to see her flash a smile at him that I haven't seen since Pa passed, and her tuck her hair into her bonnet seeming self-conscious about her appearance.

"We think it was Crows," he says, "and by the track they're headed west, so keep a sharp eye out. No reason to think they'll bother a train with this many guns, but the Crow seem to have no fear in them. Just keep an eye turned to the wilderness."

"Thanks, Captain. You fellas on the chase?"

"No, we've ranged as far from the fort as orders allow. But you may see me. I'm mustering out and headed west myself in a fortnight. I'll be on horseback with only a pack mule, so I imagine I'll overtake you folks."

"You can put your feet by our fire anytime, Captain."

"Obliged," he says. Then adds, "Cober's Canyon is only a mile or more ahead. Be damn careful in this deluge. Cox is a good man so follow his instruction. You've got over two hundred yards to winch down."

"First of many, I understand," I say with a little apprehension.

"Many have done it. Just take your time and observe caution. God speed," he says, and waves over his shoulder, pauses up beside Ma and tips his hat, then rides back to join his troop.

As we clomp forward, I can't help but notice more and more goods discarded at trailside. Tables, chairs, trunks, busted wagon wheels, churns, a pianoforte, and other items folks have decided unnecessary have been cast aside to lighten loads. Were one to establish a secondhand shop at trailside, inventory would be no problem. Of course, there would also be no customers. All would be selling, not buying.

As we pass, I hear Edna Mae exclaim, "I'd sure like to

have that pianoforte." So, I guess the girls are more observant than I thought.

Ma doesn't seem amused as she replies, "And I'd like to be Queen Victoria, which is about as likely as us taking on any more weight."

I have to smile, knowing Ma is still not particularly pleased with my older sister, although I did overhear her say she was looking forward to having another baby in the family.

In a little over a half mile from the spot of my conversation with Captain Haroldson, we pull rein as the train has stopped. I leave our wagons and ride Stubby on up ahead.

Two sturdy pines are at the edge of the precipice we're to descend, and a dozen men are already lashing lines from them to the lead wagon. I can see that many a line has been tied to the two pines, I suppose using them as anchor for block and tackle rigs. The four oxen from that wagon have been unharnessed and are being led by hand down the trail, on a serpentine stock trail that crosses back and forth over the ruts. The wagons will follow those indentations in a direct line to the bottom, where a formerly small stream now rages twenty feet wide and no telling how deep. The stream feeds into the Laramie River that is a quarter mile north of us and hundreds of feet below.

As I ride up, Cox turns from lashing the wagon. "Jake, I need that big Sampson here. This is muscle business."

"I'll help," I say.

"You'll tend to your own gear, but I need him here, so go!"

"Yes, sir."

I return past seven or eight wagons and trade places with Sampson, and he rides Stubby forward with my instruction to tie him off to the side where I can gather him up on passing. The rain has not let up and the occasional snap and crack of thunder and lightning has the stock with the whites of their eyes showing and them stomping, neighing, and bawling.

Dang if it wouldn't have been lots better to come to this spot on a bright, sunny, dry day. But that's not to be, and we're to be severely tested by this terrible obstruction.

Engstrom's wagon is ahead of us, separated by one belonging to folks I don't know. I leave Edna Mae with the pup cart, Ma seated on the big wagon, and Miss Mary and the girls afoot trying to keep the stock gathered, and I stomp through the mud up ahead to help the Engstrom's prepare.

Just as I arrive at the Engstrom's, I hear a terrible crashing, and screams reverberate back our way from the canyon's edge.

THIS TIME I RUN THROUGH THE MUD, NOW NEARLY ANKLE deep, to where men are at the edge of the precipice rigging another line. I'm sorry to see it's the Von Richter wagon, upside down, cover hoops smashed, and dangerously perched on a precipice teetering with nearly a fifty-foot vertical drop seeming a breath away. Their goods are scattered down the steep slope in front of them, and many have gone over the edge.

Erhard Von Richter is perched at the rear of the wagon, trying to use his weight to keep the fine Peter Schuttler wagon from tipping any farther, and he's yelling at the men above to hurry. His wife, Gretchen—her fist in her mouth—and their four little ones from three to twelve, are afoot and some hundred feet on down the trail, making their way in rain and ankle deep mud. Beyond them, a half dozen men, my friend Twist among them, are leading four mules, two horses, and a milk cow to the bottom.

. . .

As I'm wondering what I can do to help, Captain Cox yells at me. "Jake, on this line with us." And I hurry over to join a dozen men tending a line. I then see Sampson with its end tied around his waist and another line in hand. He jumps off the edge and into a rut and runs, slipping and sliding, only restrained by the line we're feeding out, until he reaches the Von Richter wagon, latches on, and his weight grounds it. Mr. Von Richter falls to his knees, gasping for air. Sampson hands him the other line and he fastens it around the rear axle. Immediately it's pulled back to the ruts as the men on that line draw it taut.

One of Von Richter's trunks has fallen over the edge but is caught on a stubble of brush some ten feet down from where the wagon was teetering.

Sampson signs by tapping on his chest and pointing over the edge, and I hear Captain Cox turn to the men on his line. "Give him some slack." Then almost under his breath say, "crazy som'bitch."

Sampson plunges over the side. We can't see him for a moment, then Von Richter screams, "Haul away!" We pull and Sampson appears atop the cliff dragging the small trunk.

I'm right behind Captain Cox on the line, and when Sampson is safe, he turns to me. "Von Richter did a lousy job of lashing the tongue up. It came loose, dropped into the mud as we lowered, jammed up and flipped his rig to the side." Then he yelled at all of us. "When I tell you damn fools to do something, you damn well do it and do it right. We could be burying the Von Richter's now, but we're lucky. This time."

He's hornet mad, and I understand why as Mr. Von

Richter's mistake will hold us all up, the rain is not letting up and the stream below is rising.

Captain Cox turns to us again. "I'm going down. Y'all stand by. Now, after he … after I … get his tongue lashed up, lower away. But careful. Ain't no hurry as the rest of us are likely to be here for at least the night."

This means we'll be strung out on the trail as there's no place to circle up. That's way less than ideal, with savages on the prod.

With the wagon now secure to two thick Manila lines, it only takes a quarter of an hour to reach the bottom of the canyon, but the task has just begun as there's the creek to cross. Luckily, on the far side, the slope is much less steep and winching and block and tackle is unnecessary … if we can get there.

Three wagons are across, but, by far, the majority of us remain strung out up the steep slope. Still, Captain Cox orders us to make camp best we can where we are. He and Twist and four other volunteers move their mounts, lunging across the raging stream, now belly deep on the horses, taking tents with them. As the Crow are about, the Captain doesn't want the three wagons on the far side and the Von Richter wagon on the near side of the creek, but at the bottom of the steep slope, isolated without guards.

He's informed us we'll wait until the rain lets up and the stream subsides somewhat.

We are there three days, to all of our chagrin. It's an uncomfortable camp and there's plenty of grousing and complaining, but not so much after we learn that the Von Richter's have lost three quarters of their foodstuffs and heirlooms Mrs. Von Richter's family hauled all the way from Europe.

It reminds me of one of my Pa's favorite sayings: I complained of having no shoes until I met a man with no feet.

Ma suggests we give the Von Richter's one of our steers and I agree. Particularly since Captain Cox was right, the herd is more than merely a handful to handle.

I lead him down to the bottom of the ravine and tell the Von Richters they can pay us back when we get to Oregon and find a home. He butchers the steer and Mrs. Von Richter cooks liver and onions and potatoes for all the wagon folks and the men standing guard.

Even though we barely know many of the folks in the train, it seems more and more we're becoming one big family. It seems as if one is injured, we all hurt.

One benefit of staying to outlast the weather is I have lots of time under tent canvass to get to know Amalie and to learn to play Cribbage, which she teaches with lots of laughs and smiles.

On the third day the rain stops, but the creek still roars. It's day four, early afternoon, before the creek is back to only belly deep on the horses, and the rest of us are winched down and dragged across without incident, other than one old milk cow being washed away.

Now, with luck, it's seven days or so to South Pass and the crown of the Rockies.

God willing, and, literally, the creek don't rise.

We soon leave the Laramie River, cross a long rise, and

drop to water at the Sweetwater River. And I know from my journal our next landmark.

The second day after crossing Cober's Canyon, I spot a giant blister sticking up over the hills. In the morning, if not later this evening, I'll be carving my name on Independence Rock. From my journals, I know it to be nearly a half mile long and seven hundred feet wide, a huge hump of granite.

When we make camp that evening, only a half mile from the one-hundred-thirty-foot-high blister of stone, Edna Mae, Willy, Miss Mary, Sampson and I hike to the rock and do some carving. I can see signs of folks who must be only a week or so ahead.

I carve my name not far below R. McCord, July 1, 1850. Then realize that I'm nearly fifteen years of age, if not already. I don't know today's date, but my birthday is the 8th.

Feeling a little put out as it seems no one has remembered my special day, I'm surprised when we walk back into camp and Ma has a cake with my favorite buttermilk frosting and more than a dozen folks greet me with *For He's A Jolly Good Fellow*. I turn bright red when Amalie hands me a red stocking cap she's knitted and Edna Mae a pair of calf-length socks which must have taken her half the trip to knit or crochet or whatever the ladies do. Ma fetches a wrapped package from under her bedclothes and hands it to me with, "I've been saving this since your father brought it home before we left." I unwrap it to find a note inside. It reads:

Jacob, you will soon reach your majority and I hope you reach it as a Christian man who uses his might for right, protects his mother and sisters, and follows the teaching herein. No matter what comes your way, face it head on. Love, your father.

I have to turn away as it burns my eyes with tears. I know he thought he'd be the one handing me this beautifully bound pocket-size Bible. I will treasure it.

That night, while in my hammock under the wagon, I have to wonder how many fifteen-year-olds have come halfway across the country and faced an Indian taking coup with a long spear, killed a mule thief, and been left the man of the family?

And in five more days or so, I'll cross the spine of the country and be where all water flows to the Pacific Ocean—if I don't get snake bit, scalped, or run over by my own wagon or a herd of stampeding buffalo.

I laugh to myself, then just as I'm about to fall asleep, hear some funny noises. I almost climb out to see what's making the pup cart squeak ... then I understand as I overhear some whispering, giggling, and panting.

It's Sampson and Miss Mary, and whatever they're doing takes some effort. And to be truthful, I think I know exactly what they're up to and guess I should, now that I'm fifteen.

Maybe by the time we reach Oregon they'll be entitled to claim not only three hundred twenty acres, but the six hundred forty a married couple can claim.

31

AFTER WE FINISH HARNESSING AND THE LADIES HAVE SERVED us coffee, rice and sausage for breakfast, Ma calls me aside.

"You need to speak to Mr. Sampson. Something I cannot do."

"Regarding."

"This is difficult for me to discuss with you, but here it is. Miss Mary slipped out of the wagon last night, I presumed to take care of her toilet, but that wasn't it."

"Okay," I say, but think I already know what's coming.

"She went to Sampson and I can't have the girls hearing what I think is going on between them."

I'm silent for a moment, then ask, "Just how do you suppose I broach this subject."

She sighs. "I don't want to lose Sampson. I'm fond of Miss Mary, and she's already a big help. If they're to marry in the eyes of God, then they should marry in the eyes of us here on earth, otherwise they should stay apart until they are away from the Zane family. Things are too close here for such things to be going on."

I smile tightly and nod. "When I have some private time with him, I'll broach the subject ... but he is a full-grown man."

"And I have a young daughter and one who's already been tempted by sin and will be reminded of it every day for the rest of her life. You speak with him, please."

"Yes, ma'am."

As I'm plodding along pushing the stock, waiting for Sampson to be away from Miss Mary—she's perched beside him on the big wagon—I think on what's ahead. Three days to the crown. Another ten or so headed west on the Pacific side, then north until we see the three peaks known as the Three Tetons, then west again and we'll soon come to the Snake River. We'll be following it nearly a month until the confluence of the Owyhee River, where the Snake turns due north.

We've been conservative with our money and I'm damn tired of this trail, as we all are. The rumor is that at a place called Lewiston where the Salmon River joins the Snake and there's a trading post and river port where flat boats will carry a wagon or two as far as the Willamette, only one mountain range from the sea.

We're on a long gently rising slope when I glance back to see a rider pulling a pack horse and coming at a lope, passing the wagons behind.

As I'm still concerned about slave hunters, I watch carefully as he nears. Then he swings wide to pass around our small herd, then suddenly sucks rein to a sliding stop. He's slightly past so spins back and joins me behind the stock.

"Jacob Zane," he calls out, and looks familiar to me as he gigs his horse and drags his pack horse my way.

"What the heck ..." I say, then realize is Johnathan Peabody, whose family has a farm only three miles from the one my Pa sold. And likely far more important is him who Edna Mae snuck out to see the night she became with child.

"I'm here to find Edna Mae," he mutters.

"Damn well better have brought a preacher with you," I growl back.

"If she'll have me, we'll find one."

I look over my shoulder and Edna Mae is running our way.

"Johnny, Johnny," she yells and he leaps from his horse and gathers her up in his arms.

Ma is close behind, followed by Miss Mary and Willy, and we've stopped the train behind us. Sampson is driving the big wagon but has pulled rein and is looking back our way.

Ma should look happy, to my way of thinking, but she doesn't, and she snaps, "And just what brings you this far, Mr. Peabody?"

"I've come to ask Mr. Zane for Edna Mae's hand."

"Mr. Zane passed from the cholera, so it's me you'll be askin'."

"First I gotta do this," and he fishes something out of his pocket and drops to one knee, taking Edna Mae's hand. "Will you marry me?" he asks, and she bursts into tears.

She can't speak for a minute and I can't stand the

suspense, as if I didn't know the answer. "Well," I say, "will you?"

She's nodding and crying as he slips a yellow band on her finger.

Then he turns to Ma. "Mrs. Zane, may I have your daughter's hand?"

"Well, young man, you're a bit late in asking, but yes. Seems you've ridden well over a thousand miles to ask, so I guess you're serious." She laughs, then continues, "And I happen to know we have a man of the cloth right here in this train."

"Do you happen to know which wagon?" Johnny asks.

"Jake will ride on up and help you find him."

He turns back to Edna Mae, "Is after supper too soon?"

"No, Johnny. That'll give me time to clean up if I don't stop for supper. But there's something you should know?"

He's silent for a second, looking worried, then asks, "What?"

"I'm with child."

He looks confused, then asks, "My child?"

She looks angry for a second, then laughs, "Of course your child, you dang fool."

And I'd guess it would take a shovel across his chops to get the smile off it.

That night the whole train gathers after supper, and Edna Mae Peabody gets more gifts—cloth, candles, hams, bacon, and canned fruit than we can carry in the pup cart. Then we have a real hoedown with three fiddles, a snare drum, two mouth-harps and a pianoforte. The little piano someone has unloaded for the first time, to Edna Mae's envy.

Even Captain Cox seems happy, and after downing his share of corn liquor announces, "We'll be moving off the trail and letting Hogarth pass in the morning. I won't be yelling 'wagons ho' until 10:00 a.m. So, drink up, but let me caution you, we're at six thousand five hundred feet and have one more cliff to winch up, over two hundred feet. This altitude and corn don't mix well, so take care."

The men all laugh, but as Johnny and I are driving the stock away to graze at dawn, we have to smile at all the trailsmen holding their heads and moaning. I'm feeling pretty wise for only taking a taste when Captain Cox toasted the bride and groom.

As we ride along, I ask Johnny, "You left a fine farm and are the oldest son. It'll take many a year to build such a place from the wilderness."

"Why, I plan to take Edna Mae back to Missouri."

I'm a little taken aback and chew on that a moment, then ask, "Does Edna Mae know that?"

"She's my wife. She'll do as I say."

I get a smirk, and shake my head, as I think this fellow doesn't know my sister all that well. And I'm pretty dang sure Ma won't take kindly to the idea. In fact, she may take Pa's double barrel after Johnny.

So, I mention, "You might think on that a while as Ma's looking forward to her first grandchild."

"Oh, I wouldn't try the trip with Edna Mae growing a watermelon in her belly. I'll help y'all get settled and wait until my son is at least two."

I let out a deep breath, then advise him a little more,

"Then do us all a favor and don't mention going away to Ma until y'all are nearing time, if there comes a time."

"I promised my Pa."

"Fine, just keep it to us."

Later in the afternoon, Johnny takes the reins to the big wagon and Sampson mounts Johnny's big pack horse to help me with the herd, and I have a chance to voice Ma's concerns.

"Sampson, you got me chewed on."

He gives me a curious look, obviously having no idea what I'm referring to, so I have to be more explicit.

"You and Miss Mary kept us all awake the other night. Ma says she can't have that kind of thing happening when little Willy is nearby. In fact, not at all in our camp."

He nods, looking very serious and a little embarrassed. Then he points off at a nearby wood, and makes his fingers imitate walking. Then waves both hands, indicating far away.

"That should do. You and Miss Mary take some long walks in the woods, out of sight of the wagons. In fact, I'll tell Ma that Johnny and I are taking over watering and grazing the stock and we'll be leaving firewood and chips to you and Miss Mary and that Miss Mary won't be slipping out of the wagon come midnight. That suit you?"

He nods with some vigor, and we both laugh.

I'm beginning to believe my calling may be as a politician.

Tomorrow we'll be on the Pacific side and our trip more than half over, particularly time wise if'n we catch a flat boat to cross most of Oregon Territory.

A flat boat, if it makes it through the rapids, can drop us off at the north end of the rich fertile Willamette Valley, and in some two months we'll be filing a land claim. God willing and some creek don't wash us away, or lightning kills all, or we die of thirst, or God only knows what.

So far, except for Pa, we've been lucky.

Now what? I keep waiting for the other boot to drop.

32

WE'RE HAVING TO STOP MORE AND MORE FOR BREAKDOWNS as the wear and tear of travel—bouncing along on the ruts, having to pry axles over rocks and ridges, running low on grease, and fittings and parts being used up without a source of replacement—are causing lots of stops for repair. It's also causing lots of conflict as one traveler seeks to borrow parts from another—parts that traveler may have to have himself in the near future. And not only parts, but supplies, as folks use up or lose to wrecks every sort of foodstuff and tools. More and more items thought to be precious are cast aside and the trail is littered with furniture and wooden cases that have been emptied of supplies. Wood is no longer much of a problem and we are not having to collect buffalo chips.

The Indians still shadow the trail, seeing what they can scavenge as folks dispose of the weight that seems to wear on them and wagons as we proceed.

Water has been no problem and won't be, or so I read, until we follow the Snake River west. At first thought, one would think water no problem when moving along the bank of a pure cold river, but the Snake has cut a deep canyon with vertical walls and there's no getting to the stream, particularly for stock.

I'm beginning to understand more and more why Captain Cox wanted us to butcher and salt and jerk our sheep and steers. I wish we'd done so, but still know I can't start another herd in Oregon without breed stock, and that's even more important than meat.

Ma and I spend a few grim moments after supper counting up the folks we've lost to accidents and sickness and, even after experiencing it on the trail, are surprised to count to nine: four by accident including Amalie's little sister Birgit; two to some kind of poisoning, likely something they tried to harvest from the wild; and three to cholera including Pa. We decide it is damn bad luck to lose Pa, when only three from our train succumbed to the rotten disease. In some way it was a blessing Pa passed so quickly as the other two took three and four days to die, suffering terribly, which is not only hard on the sick person but to all the folks trying to care for them and praying for them to be well.

Then, the hardest thing of all, having to leave them in the cold soil with little to mark their passing, other than memories.

Even though they are consuming supplies, I find it a blessing to have Miss Mary and Johnathan Peabody in our party. Johnny is a fine hunter and more than willing to wander into the woods, and Miss Mary is as good with a spatula and mixing bowl as are Ma and Edna Mae. And all of us are getting along fine considering the close quarters, and both Johnny and Edna Mae and Sampson and Miss Mary wanting privacy from time to time.

From the crown at South Pass, soon turning north, we're only two days to seeing the Three Tetons in the distance. If there were giants living above the ramparts of a monstrous castle they'd be in those hard shouldered, rugged crowned, snow-capped peaks. This third day from South Pass it seems the country is leveling out ahead, and there's the hope of some civilization at Fort Hall.

The third night after seeing the peaks, we're camped near a small river with what seems to be the last of the pine-covered slopes of the Rockies. Some say this is called the Wasatch Range to our north and east. As we're low on fresh meat, Johnny, Sampson, and I decide to go across the river and into the woods with the hope of bringing back a fat mule deer or, if truly fortunate, a big bull or cow elk.

It seems we're not alone as we wade the little river with water only as deep as the horse's belly—I'm now riding the gray Johnny was using as a pack horse—and Sampson still on George. I see Twist in the distance and give him a wave. We space ourselves over two hundred yards apart as we enter the copse of lodgepole pine.

I've not seen nearly so much of Twist since Johnny made his appearance and can only conclude that he had eyes for Edna Mae, and he's been busy helping with repairs and keeping folks encouraged and moving. Some seem so exhausted they're somber and a smile might break their faces.

We have a bit of a wind at our back that doesn't bode well for hunters as these deer and elk seem to smell a hunter a mile distant, if the wind be in their favor. But after a half mile or so and the climb of over five hundred feet in elevation, the wind changes. I check the sun and conjure we only have another hour to hunt before we'll have to turn and head back. Twist, if we're all still heading northwest, is only four hundred yards northwest, Sampson two hundred in the same direction, and Johnny two hundred southeast of me.

I've seen some sign of both deer and elk—tracks and scat —and am moving slowly, letting the gray pick his way to the top of a ridge, now among ponderosa pine, when I hear a shot east of me.

I rein up, waiting to hear another so I can get a good grab on direction, but there's only one.

If Johnny has something down he'll need help so I turn the gray that direction and gig him into a brisk walk, having to weave in and out of the big pines as we slightly descend.

I'm a quarter hour into trying to locate him, not wanting to call out as I may spook my own chance at meat, when I hear a shot, then another and another. Obviously, Johnny is emptying his Colt at something and the rapidity of the shots means he's not putting an elk or deer out of its misery. He's likely firing in self-defense.

I give hard heels to the gray.

It must be a bear. We been cautioned that the bears near the trail—and we've seen only three grizzly and a half dozen black bears and those at a half mile or more distance—are becoming accustomed to gunshots. Not only accustomed, but aware that a gunshot often means a gut pile. And they don't run from a gunshot, but ofttimes to one.

I bust out of the trees into a meadow, a steep one flanking

what seems to be a small stream. But the meadow is deep in grass, like the river below the grass sweeps the gray's belly.

I gig him forward, but for the first time since I've been riding him, his ears turn forward, he snorts and if ridding his nostrils of a bad odor, then shies. He takes the bit in his mouth and spins to head back into the trees. I'm jerking him hard to turn, but he won't be turned. I have his chin sucked up to his chest and he doesn't show any sign of slowing.

I pull my muzzle loader from its scabbard, throw a leg over the gray's withers and, while he's digging his legs under him to escape, drop from the saddle. Then I turn and run, backtracking the hundred feet I've lost while battling the gray.

I hear a terrible roaring, one that raises the hair on the back of my neck and sends a shiver down my backbone. Then Johnny's screams compound the shivers and my mouth goes dry.

Obviously, no longer concerned with missing an opportunity for deer or elk, I start yelling at the top of my lungs as I run into the meadow.

"Johnny! Johnny! Where are you?"

Reaching the stream which is only ankle deep, with the grass grazed down on its banks, I spin in the direction of his yelling and the bear growling and gnashing its teeth and look upstream. Only forty yards or so. I gasp at the sight. It is a grizzly and it has Johnny down, face down, trying to crawl out of the monster's grasp. Nearby is the partially gutted body of a cow elk.

Quickly I check my load as I run, closing the distance to twenty yards then bring the rifle up while I drop to one knee.

From that position, I have less chance of shooting Johnny instead of the monster.

I fire and the animal doesn't even flinch, busy as he is trying to dispatch the man. Johnny has both hands on the back of his neck, trying to get his knees under him but it's an impossible task with several hundred pounds of bear atop him.

THROWING THE RIFLE ASIDE, I PULL MY COLT AND WITH ALL the courage I can muster start forward, firing with every second step. I'd like to try a head or neck shot, but the animal is head down—its huge head nearly one with Johnny's head—and if I missed only slightly, I could put Johnny out of his misery.

To my surprise over my left shoulder another shot roars, and I take a quick look to see Sampson. He's now throwing his muzzle loader aside and palming his Colt.

The bear releases Johnny, turns his attention to us and charges, spittle flying, roaring. We're both firing. I get off two more shots before the bear is on me, but sweeps me aside, as if I was a hummingbird, and rumbles on by.

I'm on my side in the stream, gasping as I've inhaled water, trying to get back on my feet. I see Sampson with both hands on his Colt and he gets off two more shots as the slathering bear disappears into the tall grass.

Rather than worry about the bear, I stumble up through the slippery rock-strewn stream until I reach Johnny.

He's on his face in the streamside mud, unmoving. His back looks like he took one hundred lashes from a pirate captain while lashed to the mast. I reach down and carefully turn his head so he doesn't drown in the mud, and he gasps. He's alive. Hurt as badly as I've ever seen anyone ... but alive.

So far.

Sampson puts a hand on my back and it comes away bloody.

"What?" I say, surprised as if I'm hurt fear and shock is covering it nicely.

He motions unbuttoning his shirt, but I'm more worried about stopping Johnny's bleeding at the moment. I rip away shards of his shirt and pack the gashes in his back until I've done as much as possible, then hear Twist's voice yelling for us.

"Careful!" I shout back. "Big damn bear."

In moments he's at our side, and quickly peels his shirt off and tears it into strips. We have two horses, as mine and Johnny's have abandoned ship. I can't find fault with them.

"Get your shirt off," Twist commands and I do. He tears mine into long strips and binds my wound tightly around my chest.

"A deep gash with need of some sewing," he says, and adds, "and another that won't. Let's get Johnny across a horse and you can lead him down if you're up to it?"

"Hell, I barely feel it so far."

"You'll feel it all right." He turns to Sampson. "Okay with you we walk back?"

Sampson nods, then as if Johnny—who's much bigger than I am—is a feather, lifts him and carries him to big George, his mount, and with Twist calming the animal, drapes him across the saddle. He quickly ties a thigh to one side leather tie and a bicep to the other, then looks at me as if to say, "hurry."

While he's working, Twist is reloading my Colt and shoves it back in my holster.

And I do hurry mounting Twist's horse. And we set out at a brisk walk. I'm likely a half hour to the little river and yell to Ma and the girls.

I'm pleased to note Edna Mae and Willy have lead ropes on my horse and Sampson's, which have returned to camp of their own accord.

"Quick, Johnny's hurt," I yell and cross the river to where they're waiting, Edna Mae with a fist in her mouth sobbing silently, and Willy now wailing. I quickly explain to Ma what happened until she interrupts me when I turn and she sees blood has stained my backside to my knees.

"You're hurt bad," Ma says, and I admit I'm beginning to pain something fierce. But not nearly so much as when Edna Mae, keeping one eye on Ma tending to Johnny, does as Ma instructs, sets me on a log and scrubs my wounds with water and lye soap.

When she's finished scrubbing and dressing my back with clean linens, I collapse in my hammock. I hear Johnny groan as Ma goes after his back with needle and thread. Then I hear her lament, "He never gained consciousness even with the pain of the needle. Let's all pray he hasn't lost too much blood."

But I'm back up when it's turns dark. None of us have had our supper, when Sampson and Twist wade the river and come to our fire. Twist has a long loin draped over each shoulder and Sampson a hindquarter on each of his. Both have reloaded their weapons,

Twist unloads the elk loins, squats by the fire and turns to Ma. "How's Johnny?"

"He's lost so much blood," she says. "He's in the wagon with Edna Mae. I hope he makes the night." Then she adds, "And neither of you are hurt?"

Twist answers with a shake of his head. "No, ma'am. But I'll tell you, walking back with fresh meat on your shoulders knowing there's and man-killer of a monster wanting supper was not my favorite stroll."

She nods knowingly. Then walks over and checks my dressing. And even though Edna Mae can't hear, says, "Good job, young lady, but I think you're gonna need a needle and thread."

"If'n you say so," I offer, then add, "But first, I believe I'd like to try my hand at that jug of John Barleycorn Pa hid out."

She gives me a tight smile. "As long as you save a mouthful or more for me. I believe I'll need it before this night is over."

I manage several mouths full before I finally choke and can't face another.

I've had a better time than watching Willy wince every time Ma jabs a needle in my back. It is almost as bad as watching myself, but I'm glad it's my back and I can't see her work. I'm dizzy as a whirling dervish dancer, and I don't know if it's from the whiskey or the pain, but I guess the pain as I am more than eager to take another deep draw on the jug when she's done.

"Twenty-seven stitches, Mr. Zane. You're a brave patient," Ma says, then adds, "Hand me that jug. Then I'm going to roast up half that very, very, very expensive elk loin." But before she takes a swig, she pours a dollop on my wound that makes me want to do a jig, but I don't.

"Save me some for breakfast," I manage as I head back to my hammock.

I awake several times in the night, the last time, as the sky to the east is turning golden, to Edna Mae screaming and wailing.

Johnny didn't make the night. Ma thinks his neck is broken, and maybe some of his back.

By noon, we have him buried up on the hillside, with a fine headstone of a one-foot-thick granite shard chiseled by Twist and Sampson. Not even Edna Mae knows the year of his birth, but we know his age, twenty, and count backward.

It's been two days more of travelling mostly long gentle valleys, some of it along the Portneuf River. We're rumored to be near the Snake, and soon it's proven as we see Fort Hall in the distance.

As it's growing dark, Captain Cox circles the wagons and we camp with Fort Hall only two miles or so away. A number of the ladies express their resentment at being so close to a sutler and bathhouse, but Cox in nonplussed, to use one of Ma's recent dictionary words. It means 'so unaffected as to not increase one's pulse'.

There are, however, Indians about, and more than one group has been spotted travelling in unison, if at a distance, with our train.

Captain Cox seems to be particularly at ease as he informs us there's an Army Compound, Cantonment Loring, not far from Fort Hall. The fort itself was established decades ago as a trading post while the area was still in dispute with England, but in 1846, after our defeat of Mexico, the English and their Hudson Bay Company relinquished the territory to the United States.

Morning finds us nearing Fort Hall, a fairly roomy adobe structure that looks sturdy enough to repel a large force of savages. We pass a dozen teepees that are reported to be Shoshone and Bannock. Shoshone being the tribe of Sacajawea, the Indian maiden who accompanied Lewis and Clark on their great voyage of discovery.

One of their braves rides out and moves from wagon to wagon, trying to trade a bear hide for an ax head, and as I still have Pa's supply of trading material, ax heads and needles, I accommodate him. It's a large grizzly hide and I figure it's something to give Johnny's son or daughter when old enough to tell the tale of how the child's father died. In fact, the symbol of a dead bear might offer some solace. An eye for an eye.

That said, I'm sure the bear that attacked Johnny must have died. If not, he's carrying several ounces of lead.

Edna Mae has developed a nice round belly, now justified in the eyes of some of the more pious women on the train by the fact her 'husband' showed up. Ma has taken to reporting that the wedding held while travelling was merely a renewing of hurried vows taken back in Missouri. Many on the train doubt this story, but at least it's a story a child can live with rather than being branded a bastard.

And I'm worried that she might be harming her baby. She's been sobbing off and on since Johnathan passed. I'm beginning to wonder if she'll ever run out of tears.

Ma has to practically drag Edna Mae, wailing and complaining, to Fort Hall's sutler then to the bathhouse. I'm a little surprised that Miss Mary says she'll heat some water and use a washrag and stand guard at camp, while we're gone. I've taken a scrub at every water hole deep enough and by which we've camped since we left Missouri. I've passed the last several as I didn't want to reopen my wounds. Ma says she'll remove the stitches after supper if it looks healed enough. She's been checking my wounds morning, noon, and night to make sure they smell clean and are not going green. If so, she'd have to reopen and scrub them again and that might just make me pass out or throw up or some such.

I'm hoping to get rid of the catgut even though I can't imagine how much fun it will be to have her jerk the thin sewing material back through the wound. She tells me of a time when I was five and got stitches in my arm when I fell on one of Pa's hoes, but I don't remember the incident, even looking at the scar. I guess that's a good thing, me not remembering? It couldn't have been so terrible since I don't remember.

I'm a little sickened by the thought of having a rat eater's intestine used to sew me up, but Ma's laughed at me and informed me that catgut is only a name, and the thin cord is really made from a goat's intestine. I guess that's supposed to make me feel better, but I've seen some of the things goats eat and I'm not soothed.

I have enough of my thirty dollars I got from selling Jeri's horse to the reverend. The meals and a bucket of trout I saw them haul in look so good at a café in Fort Hall that I decided to treat us all to supper. We're charged as much as we would be for steak, but I don't complain as fried trout, every plate with a fourteen or more incher; yams doused in honey; sweet peas, fresh garden peas cooked with bacon; and a quarter apple pie each soothes my injured pocket book even more. I invite Twist to join us, and he does, sitting by Edna Mae and trying his best to cheer her up. I actually do see her smile one time.

I'm particularly pleased to see Captain Haroldson, no longer a captain, walk in as we're finishing our dessert.

Ma convinces me that I can go to the bathhouse and soak in a tub without getting my wound below the water level, and I convince Twist and Sampson to join me. While Captain Haroldson, whose first name I've now learned is Quentin—friends call him Quent, he informs me, and invites me to do so—offers to stay, guard the ladies and have coffee with Ma. I take him up on it. I have mixed emotions as I admire the man but am suspicious he has eyes for the Widow Zane. It makes me both smile and grit my teeth.

Then I have to refuse to bathe at all as the attendant, a fat blond man with a scraggly dirty blond beard, refuses to allow Sampson to partake.

"He's my family," I say through clenched teeth.

"No Indians or Nigras," the man says with hands on hips.

"Then no six bits," I say.

"Y'all are welcome, but not him," he says.

So, I can't help but offer, as we walk out, "It's a pleasure not doing business with you." And we all laugh.

Now I wonder if Miss Mary didn't anticipate the problem and did not want to be embarrassed. I decide to buy her and Sampson something special if something can be found at the sutlers.

Before I return to fetch Ma, Edna Mae, and Willy and bid goodnight to Quent, I drop in and find a pair of Shoshone moccasins that will fit each of them. Sampson's are nearly knee high, and both have some handsome bead work. Rather than a hot bath, I use the quarters to treat we three to a sarsaparilla. We take it to the café and join the others.

"Ask him," Ma says to Quent as I plop down.

He turns to me. "I'm headed to Oregon as well. I'm thinking I could ride along with y'all if it suits you."

I'm silent for a moment, then advise, thinking I might discourage him although I truly don't know why I would, "We got stock to graze and water, wagons to keep repaired, and hunting to do. Riding with us will sure as Hell is hot …."

"Jake Zane," Ma snaps at me.

"Sorry, Ma, man talk."

"Not around us ladies," she gives me right back.

"Sorry. Anyway, sure as the devil, it will slow you down. You could be in the Willamette likely a month before us."

"Likely," he says, and gives me a smile, "But I wouldn't have the pleasure of your company. I don't imagine it will surprise you to know I carry my weight and more. I've covered this next two hundred miles and you'll also discover water may come dear ... it may not if it rains ... but it may be a terrible challenge. So, what do you think, Jake? Can you use a tried-and-true trail hand?"

I shrug. "If Ma says it's okay, it's fine with me. I never had no problem with fewer chores."

He extends his hand. "Nice to be aboard."

I shake. I do like the man. And a man doesn't rise to be a Captain of Dragoons out here in the wilderness with wild animals, weather, and savages without being competent. Probably that and more.

Now, if we just continue to get along. We've been a family so far, and I hope we stay so.

WALKING OR RIDING A MULE OR HORSE OR EVEN BOUNCING
along in a wagon can be terribly boring, and I'm more than
happy to discover that Quent Haroldson is a fine story teller.
He's not a vain man as he's not a hero in any of his stories—
although I suspect he was a hero many times over.

As it happened, he served with General Kearny on his
march from Santa Fe, New Mexico, to California where he
engaged the *Californio* lancers at the Battle of San Pasqual,
then on into California. He actually met General Fremont,
who we learned visited Fort Hall and whose name I saw
inscribed on Independence Rock, near a tall cross it's said he
and his men carved to show the passing of Christians.

The captain rode with Kit Carson, and the tales of this
small mountain man no larger in his maturity than I am now,
are known far and wide in the West. He tells a tale of Carson
and a Navy officer, Lt. Ned Beale, who snuck through the
Mexican lines to get help from Commodore Stockton in San

Diego, and both arrived full of cactus and in terrible shape, but the Dragoons were saved by their heroism.

He tells of a marine, Archibald Gillespie, off Commodore Stockton's ship, the *Congress*, who commandeered a cannon, loading and firing by himself and saved all at the Battle of San Pasqual. Then of a man, John Brown—Juan Flaco was his Mexican name that he tells me is translated to Slim John—who rode from Los Angeles to Monterey, three hundred fifty miles, in five days. He rode one horse to death on the way, to save the Dragoons and Marines trapped in the square. A heroic ride unequaled to anyone's knowledge. He even knows the real name of Los Angeles: *El Pueblo de Nuestra Señora la Reina de los Angeles de Porciúncula* or The Town of Our Lady the Queen of Angels of the Little Portion, although its unofficial name was simply *El Pueblo de la Reina de Los Angeles*. And more simply Los Angeles. And, I'm surprised to find he speaks both Spanish and French, and fluently I discover, as he talks with another trail man who was born in Spain.

I'm truly happy to have him along, even though I'm not happy to note the way my Ma looks and him, and the looks he returns.

I'll have to chew on that.

We're five days along the Snake River, the last three of which we're south of its black lava rock canyon that is well over a hundred vertical feet deep. There is no way to reach the water. And as predicted by Quent, we're soon out. As he promised, he takes his big bay horse and drags Mark, one of the big mules, with two twenty gallon kegs on a side. He leads a dozen men from other wagons, each with pack horses or mules and even two dragging oxen. They return before noon loaded with water, and he takes another trip arriving back just before dark. We're stuck, as the stock has to have water and it's a minimum of one gallon per hundred pounds of body weight. That's six or seven gallons for each steer, more than half that again for each oxen, horse and mule.

All we're doing with eighty gallons a day is keeping them alive. We can't proceed as we'll walk our animals to death. It is so very frustrating to see millions of gallons, now over two hundred feet below, flowing by, and have your stock going thirsty.

Four of the wagons from the train decide to move forward with the hope of finding water. Quent tells us they will not—unless it rains. But he assures us we can hold on until it rains.

And he's right much sooner than I'd even hoped.

I snap awake during this moonless night and look out to discover it's starless as well. A thick overcast. I'm just dozing off again, when I hear the distant roll of thunder. I fall asleep, I'm sure, with a smile on my face. I awake to the pitter patter of rain.

Unfortunately, it's not enough to pool. We quickly put out canvas with the hope we can collect enough to keep us from having to make two trips with our two twenty-gallon kegs, but alas, no pooling and it stops soon.

"It's okay," Quent reassures us. It's raining hard in the mountains to the south. I'll bet by noon we have streams running. It takes some time to soak this lava rock, but when it's soaked, things change quickly.

And he's right. By noon, a nearby ravine is running strong.

Captain Cox rides up. "Let's move out. If we can get to the Owyhee by tomorrow noon we'll be fine."

And we pack quickly. Quent is fine driving the big wagon, and Ma seems content to ride beside him. Miss Mary likes to walk, but soon tires of the rough ground and rides the wagon box at the rear, content to read one of Pa's books. Occasionally she waves me over to explain or pronounce a word for it. It leaves Edna Mae to drive the pup cart with Willy at her side. Sampson and I to drive the stock, now that we have Johnny's horses. Stubby even gets to run with the steers and remaining sheep. We're down to three as two have disappeared. I don't know if stolen by Indians or some other hooligan, or just wandered off, which is unlikely. But whatever the reason, they're gone.

I'm half dozing in the saddle when there's a commotion in the herd. I snap to and see our remaining milk cow leaping away, and something is flopping from a foreleg.

I gig the gray I'm riding forward and see the problem. A rattlesnake, at least five feet long and thicker in the middle than my bicep, has attached itself to her leg. She's bawling like her sister did when her leg snapped. It's my understanding a rattler strikes then backs away. This one must have gotten fangs hung up in bone or cartilage.

I dismount with my Colts in hand, but she steps on the snake with her other hoof and kicks free. The snake's injured and flopping around, so rather than waste a shell, I pick up a rock the size of my head and smash its head with a single well-aimed blow.

The cow has moved off a few feet, but merely stands, panting, drooling, head down, shivering.

Quent pulls rein, dismounts the wagon, and walks back. He bends next to her and rubs the leg up and down, then gives me a look and a shrug.

"It's already swelling. She might survive, but she'll never keep up. I'd put her down and leave her for the buzzards. I would not butcher her. We got lots of meat and I'm not sure the risk of eating snake bit."

"I agree." I pull my Colt and put the muzzle behind her ear, and she drops in her tracks. Then I say, "Thanks, old cow, for all that milk and cheese and butter. Hope you're in green pastures in cow heaven."

Quent gives me a smile. "You'll make a hell of a fine rancher or farmer," he says and starts to stride back to the wagon but stops and turns again before I can mount the gray. "Hey, that fat snake will eat if you wanna mess with it."

I shake my head and let him lie.

Captain Cox shows up, wondering about the gunshot, and I wave him off with a, "Snake-bit cow. Put her down."

"Big snake?" he asks, and I give him my arms stretched wide.

"You keep him?" he asks.

"No, sir," I reply.

"Mind if I pick him up?"

I laugh. "Maybe it'll sweeten you up, a good ol' poison critter like that."

"You're getting a real sense of humor, younger," he says, but laughs as he goes for the snake.

Tomorrow, after we cross the Owlhee River, we follow the Snake as it turns due north, then we're only a few days to Lewiston and the river port where we make up our mind to risk the riverboat.

WE LOSE ANOTHER SHEEP ON THE OWLHEE, RUNNING HARD and fast with the recent rains, which have come nightly.

The Snake River canyon is no longer nearly vertical. But the trail is three-eighths to one-half mile above the river, and the banks and mountain on the west of the river are nearly forty-five degrees. There's no getting wagons down and it would take most of a day to get the stock down and back.

But there's the intermittent stream, and belly-deep graze within a half mile to the west of the trail. The country to the west is gentle and rolling, and to be truthful, I'm wondering why a farmer would need to go all the way to the Willamette Valley.

As we make supper looking at a beautiful yellow, orange and blue sunset in the west, I question Ma and Quent.

"I'll tell you, we still have the makin' of a cattle herd. If I can trade a couple of steers for a cow, and a couple of ewes for a ram, and maybe trade the big wagon for a few head, we'd be off and looking at some stock to sell in a couple of years—steers and rams anyway."

"What are you saying," Quent asks, and Sampson is nodding.

"I'm saying this country west of the Snake looks beautiful to me. Deep grass...."

"There's a land agent in Lewistown, only another day's ride."

"And this is land claim country?" I ask.

"Heck, boy, as far as you can see."

Edna Mae speaks up. "Twist has asked me for my hand, in a year or so, after a decent time since Johnny ... since Johnny...."

"Maybe Twist would consider staying hereabouts?" I ask

Ma stands from the log she's perched upon and stares off to the west, then turns to Quent. "Did you want to speak with Jake?"

"I do. Jake, how about you and I take a stroll so we can chat?"

I sigh deeply, suspecting what's coming and both looking forward to and fearing this conversation.

We've only gone two dozen steps toward a drop-off overlooking the Snake far below, when he puts a hand on my shoulder, and says, "I suspect you know what this is about. You're not blind."

"I suspect."

"Your mother and I have come to care for each other. She won't consider marrying until your Pa has passed for more than a year ..."

I guess I've made up my mind about Quent, so I interrupt,

"I think that's an old-fashioned notion, on both Ma and Edna Mae's part. Far as I'm concerned that's a city notion, and we're in the wilderness and must take on wilderness ways. And longtime courtin' ain't much use out here. If you don't know a fella's notions, or a lady's for that matter, after a month of hardship, you likely never will."

He gives me a pat on the shoulder then takes my shoulders in both hands and looks me in the eye. "Mr. Zane, you're way older than your years."

"Captain Haroldson, if the Oregon Trail doesn't put some years on you, I don't know what would."

"Then is this the place?"

"I suggest we stop in Lewiston, talk to the land agent, make sure this is Claim land, then let the train go off if they're a mind to. I want to have a talk with Mr. and Mrs. Engstrom and find out where they plan to light. When I reach my majority, I plan to see what the status is of their daughter Amalie."

"A sweet girl."

"And I need to talk with Twist. My sister looks at him like he's hard candy. Maybe he'd like to hang around. If Twist and I told a small white lie and said we were eighteen, old enough to file, I guess you could look the other way?"

"Hell, I'll witness for you. Last I knew you turned eighteen back on the trail."

"In the morning, afore the others are about, how about you and I riding out west a little and see the lay of the land."

"Maybe we can drop an elk. I saw a herd of over a hundred off in the distance this afternoon."

"Sounds good, neighbor." We both laugh at that, for if all

of us file, we'll have dang near two sections. "You know what two sections of land would cost in Missouri."

"Lots of money, lad. Lots of money. But to tell the truth, you folks have paid plenty to come west, and not only in dollars. And the paying may not be over before we're all comfortable in front of our own fire."

"But whatever it is, it'll be ours."

As we walk back, I'm thinking, I wish he was Pa, but he ain't, and I like and respect him, so that's that. And we're here with thousands of acres of rich grassland, some soon to be farmland, off to the west. We got a river that will served as a highway all the way to Portland. We got timber to build with and to sell, should we find a market. We got elk and deer to fill the larder. We got seeds, and we know how to farm. And we got a town nearby.

And we got each other.

While Ma drives the pup cart and Sampson the big wagon, Quent and I make a wide pass to the west of the river where we cross hills deep in meadow grass that means they'd be deep in planted wheat, barley and corn. The ground looks as if it would support nearly any crop and by the tree cover most orchard trees. And there's elk and deer for the taking. And nearly every ravine runs with a clear water creek.

The Snake is growing into a real river, over one hundred paces across when we reach the bank opposite the village of Lewistown. It's situated on the east side of the Snake and south side of the Salmon, where they converge.

As we're on the west side, we circle the wagons and plan to take the small ferry across in the morning.

Captain Cox joins us at supper time and informs me he is

friends with Farley Snodgrass, who owns half the village and is the land agent. He says it's time for the train to lay over a day so folks can make repairs and use the smithy in town, if needed, and he says there's a decent mercantile as well.

He offers to accompany us into town and introduce us to Snodgrass.

There's a fair chance we're home.

As Captain Cox is doing us the favor of an introduction, I pay his dime and that of Sampson and Miss Mary to cross. Captain Haroldson is with us and insists on paying his own way. We're at the ferry landing just after sunup and have to wait for the ferryman to arrive and pole over.

Lewistown is a small but active village as folks are already moving around. The main business seems to be a water-driven lumber mill on the banks of the Salmon River. Two dozen houses, a saloon—Two River's Water Hole—and a mercantile, hotel, boarding house are the primary businesses on Front Street along the Snake River. Scattered about is a livery, a saddlery, and a bakery and café. The most substantial building is a thin stone two-story affair with a sign reading *Farley Snodgrass, Esq., Land Agent, Attorney, Undertaker & Mayor of Lewiston, Oregon Territory*. I'm impressed with his many talents—of course, it is his sign.

The front door, flanked by tall windows, opens directly

onto his single office with a narrow stairway leading to the second floor, marked private. I presume his living quarters.

"Welcome, gents," he says and steps out from behind his desk, then realizes he recognizes Cox and extends his hand. "Captain Cox, another successful crossing, I see." He also shakes with me and Captain Haroldson, but ignores Sampson and Miss Mary. They seem unbothered by the slight. It riles me a little, but I'm here for a purpose—not to argue or insult.

"So far," Cox says.

"What brings y'all here?"

"The Land Claim act," Cox says.

There are only three chairs, other than the one Snodgrass had occupied, but he says, "Sit, sit."

Sampson remains standing.

Snodgrass returns to his chair. He's a balding man with far too much hair on the sides and back, which he smooths after plopping in his ladderback chair. He winces as he plops down and I presume he has some affliction that pains him.

"So, Horatio, you're wanting to make a claim?"

"I'm moving on, as usual. My young friend here, his mother and her new husband, his sister, and Mr. Sampson and Miss Mary here all want to file. Another hand of mine, Tristan McGillicutty, will fulfill his contract with me when we reach the Willamette and will be back. Mr. Zane here has agreed to mark out his section …."

"Section? McGillilcutty's a married man?"

"He will be when he brings in his application."

"I guess since you been on the trail, you don't know of Portland?"

"Portland," Cox asks.

"Yep, at the north end of the Willamette they done founded a new town. There was some argument about naming her after Boston, Massachusetts, or Portland, Maine, so they flipped a coin and Portland won out. Should be at least the makings of a town there by the time you arrive. I'm informed the land office for that area will be in Portland."

"If we're not careful, the West is gonna be as over-crowded as the East," Cox says with a sigh.

Snodgrass gives me an up-and-down gaze then eyes Cox. "Your young friend here don't look old enough to file. You know you gotta be eighteen?" Then he turns to me. "You eighteen, son?"

"Mr. Snodgrass," I say, acting as if I'm taken aback, "I'm the man of my family with two sisters and a Ma to watch over and care for. Not to speak of oxen and steers and sheep and horses and mules. At least until my Ma marries up. I just led them here all the way from St. Joe, and I resent …."

"Calm down, young man. No offense meant."

Captain Cox gives him a guffaw and slaps his thigh. "Hell, Farley, this man stood up to the weather, the savages, the damnable wilderness …."

"All right, all right. He looks eighteen to me."

I guess that's settled, and I don't have to lie, just avoid answering.

But Snodgrass continues, "And you know you got to be a citizen of these United States to file, and these here Negras can't be citizens."

I'm surprised that Captain Cox speaks before I can. "By all that's holy, this man did more to get us this far than any man on the train. And this lady escaped that six-wagon massacre back this side of Fort Laramie. I'll be witness for him, for Mr. Zane, and for McGillicutty. I presume you'll take a recent captain in the United States Army at his word. If all that ain't good enough for you then ...."

"All right. Where exactly are you all filing? We need a survey and some corner markers."

"Out west of here, southwest actually. Odds are four or five miles west of the river. Mr. Zane is a capable man and dang near an engineer. He'll bring you accurate papers and maps with good corner markers."

"Some fine country out there, and no filings as of yet," Snodgrass says, then rises and walks to a map on the wall. "Here's the creeks coming from over yonder. I suggest you make a sketch of this here map and go over yonder, use them east-west creeks as rough markers and stack some cairns on the corners. Do y'all know what a section of land is?"

"Six hundred forty acres," I reply. "A mile square. A mile being five thousand two hundred eighty feet. One thousand seven hundred sixty-three foot paces. Three hundred twenty rods." I'm happy we've been studying all the way from Independence.

He laughs. "Dang if you don't know. And the government prefers you keep her square and your lines true north and south and east and west. I got a compass I'll sell you ...."

Cox interrupts him. "Got my own, thank you, Farley."

"Humph," he says, but continues. "Deviation is nineteen degrees at this latitude so your north south lines will be three hundred-forty-one degrees. That'll be true north."

"I know the three, four, five rule to establish ninety

degree square corners and she'll be square as your grandpa's outhouse. How much for the compass?" I ask.

"Fourteen dollars."

"That's too dang much," Cox says, but I speak over him.

"I'll take it," I say, and turn to Captain Cox. "You may need your'n the rest of the trip. And I was taught, never a borrower or a lender be." And I give him a wink, acknowledging it's twice what I should pay, but I want to keep Mr. Snodgrass happy. Very happy.

The Captain gives me a smile and a nod. "So," Cox clarifies, turning back to Snodgrass. "Zane here will be entitled to three hundred twenty acres; his Ma and her new husband, six hundred forty; and the Sampsons, six hundred forty? McGillicutty will also be claiming a six forty as he's hitching up with Mr. Zane's sister."

"Yes, sir," Snodgrass says. "I'll be collecting a ten-dollar filing fee for every three twenty, payable in gold coin."

Cox stands, and his voice sinks an octave. "Farley, that's a handsome sum. But you move this along and you'll get no conflict from me. I'm taking my train on to the Willamette. Portland, I guess. I'll be back late winter, weather permitting, and I'll expect all this long settled."

"I get my fee; these folks get their claims."

They shake hands and we head for the door, but Snodgrass stops us short. "Mr. Zane, I'll expect you to handle things on your side for all you folks. I'd prefer if I didn't see the Sampsons back in my office. Nor do I want them saying a thing about getting a claim. It would cause questions I don't want to face. Questions of citizenship and such. Understand?"

I turn to Sampson. "Okay with you, Mr. Sampson?" I ask, and he nods.

Snodgrass continues. "Claims will be filed in the nation's capital. Ain't no questions about color on the forms as we got no Black citizens, so let's keep all this to ourselves."

I walk over and shake hands with the claims agent. "It all stays right here in this room. I'll see you with some parcels marked out before a week's out."

He hands me four sheaves of papers. "Here's your applications. The Sampsons only need one, and one for you, and one for your Ma and her new man, and one for this McGillicutty and your sis. Y'all will have a regular kingdom out yonder. See you in a week. Come with seventy dollars in cash, gold coin if'n you would."

"Sixty, for now. McGillicutty will be paying when he files on his return."

"Fair enough," Snodgrass says, and bids us farewell.

As we mount up and head back to the ferry, Captain Cox fills me in.

"There ain't no ten-dollar filing fee per three twenty, it's five dollars, but under the circumstance."

I give him a smile. "If'n it gets the job done. I don't feel in a position to argue. Fact is, and I'm sure this goes for Sampson, I never imagined having my own three twenty and a Ma with six forty. When Twist gets back, we'll have three and a half sections of fine land. God bless America, and God bless you, Captain Cox."

"All of us," Cox says, and gives me a grin.

That night, Captain Cox and Twist have supper at our wagons. I can't help but ask, now that we're about to part ways. "Way back on the trail, where those Indians had a bridge and we paid to cross, I saw them hand you a fair amount of money. Can I ask …?"

He laughs. "So, you were thinking I was taking a cut, a bribe, for the train paying for using their bridge?"

"All I know is what I saw."

"That's old Chief Cripple Buffalo. I owed him for saving my life and loaned him the money for axes and saws so they could build that bridge and he was paying me back. If you'll recall, I gave y'all the option of crossing downstream."

I chew on that a minute, then extend my hand. "I'm sorry if I doubted you. I've learned a lot on this trip, and a good part of what I've learned is thanks to you. Please don't pass this way again without filling your belly at our table."

He laughs. "Are we gonna have another shindig, seems a couple of folks need marrying up before y'all fill out them forms, and I witness them."

It's Ma's turn to speak. "Captain Haroldson and I are ready." Then she turns to Sampson and Miss Mary and asks, "How about you two?"

They both nod.

"Thank God for that," Ma says, and both Sampson and I laugh.

I realize, after as long as I've known him and as much as we've been through, I don't know Sampson's last name. So, I ask him.

He gives me a shrug, and a smile, then leans over and gives Miss Mary a kiss on the cheek.

"We'll need a last name for the papers?" I say, a little perplexed.

"How about West?" Miss Mary says, and looks to Sampson.

He nods, and smiles, and we all laugh. I only wish Pa was here to laugh with us.

Tomorrow, we begin to mark out our new homes.

AUTHOR'S NOTE

Between 1840 and 1890, 400,000 folks crossed the plains on the Oregon-California trails in wagons, afoot, horseback, or pushing hand-carts. Forty thousand of those flocked to the trails during the gold rush year of 1849. After only ten years of traveling the trail, it averaged eleven graves per mile—mostly due to accident and disease, cholera being predominant.

This is a fictional account of one young man and his family, who set out to distance themselves from the conflict in the part of the country that became a Civil War hotbed, and of the trials and tribulations that family faced—typical of those Argonauts who sought only to make their lives better. This story is fiction, but based on dozens of journals, autobiographies, and reports.

This story only touches on a very few of the actual hardships of the trail.

On September 27, 1850, the Donation Land Claim Act of 1850 came into being. The act created a land-grab incentive for settlement of the Oregon Territory by offering 320 acres, at no charge, to qualifying adult U.S. citizens; 640 acres to married couples. Applicants were required to occupy their claims for four consecutive years. Changes in 1853 and 1854 continued the program, but lopped the size of allowable claims by fifty percent.

Only a small number of Americans resided in Oregon country before 1830, and these were mostly fur trappers—and those mostly Canadians—and missionaries who lived alongside the Indian population. But by the 1840s, government support of western expansion encouraged the coming flood of migration into Oregon territory. To encourage settlement, Congress passed the Distribution-Preemption Act of 1841, which recognized squatters' rights and allowed settlers to claim one hundred sixty acres of land. After occupying and improving the property for fourteen months, a claimant could purchase the property at one dollar and twenty-five cents per acre. The United States government hoped to establish a strong claim of settlement in Oregon country, which at that time was held jointly by the United States and Great Britain.

In 1843 white settlers in the Willamette Valley drafted a constitution and, by a vote of fifty-two to fifty, established a provisional government. Settlers could now claim up to 640 acres of land at no charge, although no treaties had been signed with the Indians.

Population growth was steady—not to speak of our defeating Mexico and acquiring many thousand citizens—and helped bring about a boundary treaty between the U.S. and Britain in 1846 that established a borderline at the 49th parallel and gave the United States claim to the territory. The U.S. had been claiming territory to ten degrees above that line, and Canada to ten degrees below, so it was a compromise pleasing both sides. Oregon Territory was officially formed on August 14, 1848, two years after our war with Mexico and our possession of their lands north of the current border. But with the territory being formed, land grants recognized under the provisional government were cancelled, the provisional governing board had been partially composed of British subjects. Settlers needed and demanded title to the parcels of land they had traveled those two-thousand-rough-and-dangerous, five-or-more-months of Oregon Trail miles, to obtain.

Oregon Territory's first Congressional representative, Samuel Royal Thurston (1816-1851), took on the land issue as his first legislative effort, convincing Washington D.C. legislators of the almost unlimited growth potential of the Pacific Northwest and the need to formulate binding property rights in the Territory. Thurston authored the Donation Land Claim Act of 1850. It recognized past claims granted under the provisional government, created the Office of Surveyor-General, and made land grants to new settlers. The Donation Land Claim Act spurred a huge land rush into Oregon Territory by offering qualifying citizens free land. Blacks, until the end of the Civil War, were not considered citizens. For the purpose of population count—thus the number of Congressmen a state could have—a slave was counted as 3/5ths of a person.

The act took effect on September 27, 1850, granting 320 acres of federal land to white male citizens eighteen years of age or older who resided on property on or before December 1, 1850. If married before December 1, 1851, the couple received an additional 320 acres in the wife's name. A large number of marriages took place during this one year to take advantage of that largess. Claimants agreed to live upon and cultivate the claim for four years, which could be counted retroactively. A certificate was issued to the claimant, granting immediate ownership once the land was occupied. Claimants who located on property between December 1, 1850, and December 1, 1853, (later extended to 1855) could obtain 160 acres of land (320 acres to married couples). Under an extension of the act in 1854, land could be purchased for $1.25 an acre. This policy held until Congress authorized the Homestead Act in 1862.

Early pioneers who settled before the act was passed, normally surveyed their own land or hired others poorly trained as surveyors. The difference in determining true- and magnetic-north descriptions was clearly understood by surveyors, but was often misunderstood by the pioneers, and in 1855 the difference between the two exceeded nineteen degrees. Section 3 of the Donation Claim Act set a clear limit of $8 a mile for surveyors' fees, but this often was ignored. Since claims needed to conform to government standards (and only surveyors recognized by the Surveyor-General were those employed by him), claims surveying became something of a racket, and excessive charges were common. Settlers became outraged at this practice, which eventually led to dismissal of the first Surveyor-General.

Most of the claims under the Donation Land Claim Act were located in the Willamette, Umpqua, and Rogue River valleys. By 1856, more than 7,000 settlers had acquired more than 2.5 million acres of property.

My thanks to Wikipedia for much of the historical information above, and to the authors of dozens of biographies, autobiographies and journals for the seeds of this tale. My undying admiration for those tough folks who made this crossing. They were the best of the muscle, brains, hide, hair, and bone of American pioneers.

ABOUT THE AUTHOR

L. J. Martin is the author of over three dozen works of both fiction and non-fiction from Bantam, Avon, Pinnacle and his own Wolfpack Publishing. He lives in, and loves, Montana with his wife, NYT bestselling romantic suspense author Kat Martin. He's been a horse wrangler, cook as both avocation and vocation, volunteer firefighter, real estate broker, general contractor, appraiser, disaster evaluator for FEMA, and traveled a good part of the world, some in his own ketch. A hunter, fisherman, photographer, cook, father and grandfather, he's been car and plane wrecked, visited a number of jusgados and a road camp, and survived cancer twice. He carries a bail-enforcement, bounty hunter, shield. He knows about what he writes about, and tries to write about what he knows.

Find more great titles by L. J. Martin and Wolfpack Publishing at: http://wolfpackpublishing.com/l-j-martin/

Made in the USA
San Bernardino, CA
19 May 2019